have a nice life

(start here)

by
Scarlett MacDougal

AlloyBooks

ALLOYBOOKS

Published by the Penguin Group

Penguin Putnam Books for Young Readers,

345 Hudson Street, New York, New York 10014, U.S.A.

Penguin Books Ltd, 27 Wrights Lane, London W8 5TZ, England

Penguin Books Australia Ltd, Ringwood, Victoria, Australia

Penguin Books Canada Ltd, 10 Alcorn Avenue, Toronto, Ontario, Canada M4V 3B2

Penguin Books (N.Z.) Ltd, 182-190 Wairau Road, Auckland 10, New Zealand

Penguin Books Ltd, Registered Offices: Harmondsworth, Middlesex, England

Published by Puffin Books,

a division of Penguin Putnam Books for Young Readers, 2000

1 3 5 7 9 10 8 6 4 2

Produced by 17th Street Productions,

an Alloy Online, Inc. company

33 West 17th Street

New York, NY 10011

Alloy, Alloy.com, AlloyBooks, and 17th Street Productions and associated logos

are trademarks and/or registered trademarks of Alloy Online, Inc.

ISBN 0-14-131020-0

Printed in the United States of America

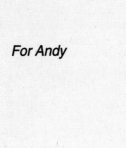

For Andy

① (Enter Fairy Godmother)

Clarence Terence didn't even hear the police siren behind him. He was trying to clear his mind so he could focus on his mission. There was nothing like the feel of the leather seat beneath you and the seconds rushing past you like trees along the highway. All of life's moments lined up before you like the broken yellow line on the highway. Follow the yellow dotted line, he told himself. Follow the yellow brick road, Dorothy. Not that he usually called himself Dorothy.

"Pull the bike over," the cop's voice blared. Clarence Terence didn't know whether to laugh or cry. After everything he'd been through he couldn't believe he was going to have to deal with some moronic Wisconsin state trooper. It was like something out of the movie *Fargo*.

Clarence pulled his motorcycle over to the side of the highway. He would go along with this for a little while, but if it took too long, he would simply have to leave. He took a

1

few deep breaths. He would not get angry at the stupid cop, but he had come all this way for the greater good, and he wasn't going to let anything stand in the way of his mission.

The cop approached the bike slowly. He was about five feet tall and pudgy, with a tiny sprout of yellow hair on top of his head, like a smudge of ballpark mustard. His name tag read Officer Shawn.

"What's that?" Officer Shawn asked, pointing to the guitar strapped to Clarence's back.

"It's a gui-tar," Clarence said slowly, as if he were talking to a small child with learning disabilities. "It's an acoustic guitar that used to belong to Eric Clapton, before he joined the Yardbirds."

"Well, okay, then. Are you aware you have some violations here?" the cop said in a thick Wisconsin accent.

Clarence looked down at his smoking bike. He couldn't very well explain to the copper that the bike had started to give him trouble in the Secpterian Galaxy when he was still thirty-three light-years away from Earth. The problem with these old bikes was every time you squeezed the brake, the bike pulled to the right. This one was definitely no Harley-Davidson, but it was hard to get a bike with integrated acceleration that could make it from galaxy to galaxy.

"I hit some ice storms and the engine started chugging," Clarence Terence said.

"Ice storms? In June?" the cop asked. He shook his

head. Clarence could tell the cop was thinking he had another nut job on his hands. One of those crazy musicians.

The cop took out his ticket pad. "Name?" he asked.

"Clarence Terence."

Officer Shawn looked him up and down.

"What's your occupation, Mr. Terence?" he asked.

Clarence thought for a moment. "Fairy godmother," he said.

The police officer stopped writing on his little pad. "I beg your pardon?"

"Fairy godmother," Clarence repeated.

Clarence Terence liked to refer to himself as a fairy god*mother* instead of a god*father* because god*father* sounded a little too *Good Fellas* meets *Cinderfella*. A little too menacing and stale. He was a mentor, a teacher, a guide. But he didn't want to put something that mundane on his intergalactic ID card. So he decided to go with fairy godmother, even though it was slightly femme.

"Yeah. It's kind of like *It's a Wonderful Life* meets *Terminator II*," Clarence Terence said. "I'm here to show four high school seniors their futures so they can fulfill their karmic destinies and I can finally redeem my sixth incarnation."

"Is this a joke?" the cop asked with a goofy smile, looking over his shoulder as if he expected a television crew to jump out from behind the bushes. "You look familiar. Are you some kind of rock star guy?"

"No," Clarence said. He got that all the time. "I'm a fairy godmother." He sneezed. Earth was terrible for his allergies.

"Oh yeah?" the cop said, raising his yellow eyebrows. "What's *my* future look like, then?"

Clarence rolled his eyes. You give some people an inch. . . . What did this cop think, that he was some kind of one-man psychic hot line? Did he have a 970 number he wasn't aware of? Did he look like Dionne Warwick? This guy was a real *schnorrer.* That's Yiddish for a real mooch.

"I've been having some problems with my wife," Officer Shawn added, suddenly sounding desperate. It was kind of sad.

"Sorry, I've got to get going," Clarence said. "I'm sure everything will work out all right." There was really no point in telling the cop that his wife was right at that moment strolling on the isthmus hand in hand with a man wearing a Madison Gas and Electric uniform.

"All right, then I need to call you in to headquarters," the cop said impatiently. "Wait here."

But Clarence Terence didn't have time to wait. He had to get to La Follette High in time for the prom.

He released the brake on his bike and kick started it with the heel of his burgundy leather over-the-knee biker boot. The cop was back in his car, talking on his radio and writing on his pad. He didn't even see Clarence leave.

②

(Featuring . . .)

Clarence liked cows. They chewed their cuds and stared and were very Zen. But after passing dairy farm after dairy farm and breathing in enough methane stink of manure and silage to last at least one lifetime, he was glad to get into the greater Madison area. Exiting off I-94 onto Route 151 by the East Towne Mall, he caught up with a red Subaru with four seventeen-year-old girls riding in it. They were singing along to an old Madonna song blasting from the radio. *When you call my name, it's like a little prayer. . . .*

How appropriate, Clarence thought. It was one of his favorite songs.

When the song ended, a female DJ came on and said, "Tonight is prom night for the graduating class of La Follette High School, so all you La Follette seniors better hurry up and pin on those corsages and put on your dancing shoes because this is WIBA 101.5 FM, telling you all to make it a good one." "It's Raining on Prom Night" came across the airwaves, making Clarence Terence feel surprisingly sentimental.

He was only a few hundred yards away from the Subaru, but he didn't want the girls to see him yet. First he wanted to review his choice, just to be sure these four girls were the right ones for him. As he cruised behind them, he activated the deluxe intergalactic View-Master that was built into his bike helmet.

"Hello, Zola Mitchell."

Suddenly there was Zola, no longer in the Subaru but standing in a cemetery while a casket was being lowered into the ground. A tall man with sandy brown hair and a golf tan was standing beside her, dressed in a black suit. He looked bewildered and kept patting his pockets like someone who had misplaced his wallet. Holding Zola's hand was a boy about eight years old, who looked like a miniature Zola—her little brother, Nathaniel. His legs were twisted around each other like he had to pee and he was talking to himself in that freaky way kids do. Zola let go of Nathaniel's hand and kissed her father on the cheek. Then she asked the minister if she could be alone at the grave. The minister touched her father's arm, and he took Nathaniel's hand and everyone walked back to their cars. Zola tucked her dark brown bob behind her ears and sat on the ground, leaning back against a mound of dirt. She stared up at the sky with her big brown eyes. Around her neck was a string of pearls, and she touched them, looking very spiritual. It reminded Clarence of that scene in *Truth or Dare* when Madonna visits her mother's grave. Except in the movie Madonna had looked innocent and sad and sexy. But Zola just looked angry. She *was* angry. Jaded at seventeen. Beautiful, and so alone. She was the star of her own sad movie.

Clarence felt his eyes welling up and he pulled the lever on the View-Master. Suddenly there was Min, short for Wilamina. He chuckled. What a ham. Min had a long brown ponytail and the cutest, smiliest, dimpliest face he'd ever seen. She was Rhoda from *Mary Tyler Moore* meets Rhoda from *Rhoda,* only part Asian. Min was riding in her boyfriend Tobias's Jeep, chomping on french fries and feeding them to Tobias, who was sitting beside her. It was their first real date and they were on their way back from the pound where they'd adopted a little Yorkshire terrier called Ozzy, their new baby. Ozzy was sitting in Tobias's lap. It had been love at first sight. Tobias and Ozzy had licked each other's noses through the metal cage, and after he'd signed all the adoption papers, they went through the McDonald's drive through to get Ozzy a Happy Meal—a hamburger and a Pokémon toy. Min thought it was incredibly romantic. Tobias was finishing up his freshman year at U Wisconsin, and Min was thrilled to be dating someone so mature.

"I bet you're going to be a great father one day," Min told Tobias ecstatically.

"Don't tell me you're one of those girls who's obsessed with having children," Tobias said, looking annoyed. He cradled Ozzy in his arms and chewed one end of a french fry while Ozzy chewed the other end. Their mouths met in the middle. "Besides, we don't need another baby," he said, gazing lovingly into Ozzy's doggy eyes.

To Clarence, the whole Min-Tobias-Ozzy thing was a little nauseating. Tobias was a jerk and Ozzy seemed like the kind of dog who would pee on your stuff if you left him alone for five minutes. But no matter what galaxy you come from, when a girl likes a guy there's not much anyone can do about it. It's a karmic thing. Clarence pulled the lever on the View-Master once more.

Olivia Dawes—or, as Clarence liked to call her, Olivia Does—reapplied her lipstick, using the glass doors of the bio lab cabinet as a mirror, and adjusted her orange halter top. She'd just finished doing it with Biology Bill Buchanan in the lab closet. Even though they didn't have two words to say to each other, Olivia couldn't get enough of Bill. She was sort of the Monica Lewinsky of La Follette High. Smart guys turned her on. Test tubes, petri dishes, and frog parts were sexier to her than champagne, a hot tub, and a Barry White CD.

Clarence sighed. He didn't get her, but Olivia would probably have a hard time getting him, too.

Olivia picked up her umbrella and walked outside to the school parking lot. It was a sunny day, but Olivia always carried an umbrella with her just in case it rained. She couldn't risk getting her hair ruined when a woman named Esperanza at the Hair Today Salon had to pull at it with a flat brush and scald it with a hot blow-dryer for a whole hour twice a week. Olivia had a different hair color practically every week. Now it was sort of Jennifer Aniston beige. A Pepperidge Farm Goldfish meets a baked, not fried Triscuit. Olivia was always changing her look. Clarence admired her skill at reinventing herself, especially when she was limited to Madison's mall stores. That took real determination and great fashion sense. But he wondered if Olivia even remembered what her natural hair color was.

Clarence pulled the View-Master lever again and ah, his favorite.

Sally Wilder was Harriet the Spy meets Laura Ingalls in *Little House on the Prairie*. Naive and smart and a great storyteller, but way too up in her head. A truckload of gorgeous, shirtless firefighters inviting her to join them for a pot of homemade chili wouldn't bring Sally down from her own private tree house. Her parents had gotten divorced when she was twelve, and that's when Sally had started writing in her diary. It had brought her through three of her mother's boyfriends, a trip to London, two summers away at theater camp in Maine, her one and *only* kiss, eleven crushes, and hundreds of fights with her mother.

In the scene in the View-Master it was nighttime. Sally stood on the lawn behind her house in her nightgown, her pale hair shining in the moonlight. She turned her diary over and over in her hands, examining it. It was a beautiful Chinese diary with a burgundy leather binding and a yellow silk cover with little Chinese trees and houses and a stream. The pages were lined and had faint pictures in the corners of fish and birds and sunsets and Chinese girls with parasols. She had filled up almost the whole thing with her neat, tiny handwriting.

But now that her mother had read it, it was ruined. She opened the lid of the garbage can and stood in the dark, ripping page after page out of the thick diary. She ripped each page into little pieces. Some of the bits blew away and scattered on the lawn but Sally kept tearing and tearing. She swore through her tears that she would never write in a diary again.

But she does, Clarence knew. She keeps a diary for the rest of her life.

Clarence clicked off the View-Master and raised the helmet on his visor. He didn't need to see any more. His maternal instinct had kicked in the moment he first saw these girls. They were irresistible; that's why he'd picked them. There was no question about it—they were meant for him, and he was meant for them. It was in the stars.

Clarence was still following the Subaru, but now that he was here, he knew he needed a game plan. It wasn't like he could just pull them over and *tell* them they needed to change their lives before they screwed up their futures. He'd have to *show* them. That's the problem with the TV generation, Gen E. Generation E! Entertainment Television, Clarence thought. It wouldn't be enough to *tell* them their futures are like *Trainspotting* meets *Dawn of the Living Dead*. He'd have to put on a song and dance and turn their futures into small indie features. Seeing is believing, as they say.

③

(**Narrow Landing Strip**)

Min pulled the red Subaru into her driveway and she, Zola, Olivia, and Sally all climbed out, holding their prom gowns and shopping bags full of shoes and various accessories. She was anxious for them to get upstairs to her room so they could start getting ready. Hopefully her dad wouldn't make a big deal out of it being prom night and start crying and taking pictures. He could get like that sometimes. Min was adopted, and her parents got excited over every little thing she did. She also got to do pretty much anything she wanted. Min was half Vietnamese (other half unknown), and Zola had a theory that Min's parents were bearing the burden of their *Kollektivschuld* over the Vietnam War, so they outdid themselves to keep Min happy.

"Come on, let's get the show on the road," Min said, walking quickly toward the house. She turned around to find Sally struggling with her giant Burdines garment bag.

Sally suddenly stopped and looked at Min and the others.

"Do any of you feel strange?" Sally asked. "I just had the weirdest sensation, almost like I'm being watched."

"You're just nervous because you have an actual date," Zola said.

They went into Min's house and straight up to her bedroom, which was all Martha Stewarted out thanks to her mom. The room was perfectly decorated with flowery bedding and dozens of pillows and was really pretty nice except for the shelf of dolls from around the world that her grandmother had given her over the years and her parents wouldn't let her get rid of. There was an African doll with beaded hair, an Eskimo doll in fur boots, a Scottish doll in a plaid kilt, and a Japanese doll in a silk kimono. There was every damn kind of doll you could imagine in every kind of outfit. Just once, Min wished her grandmother would give her money like everyone else's. The only thing about Min's bedroom that was really her own was the poster-size blowup of Ozzy on the wall.

Min looked at the digital clock on her VCR. She thought they had given themselves plenty of time but somehow it was already almost six o'clock and their dates were supposed to be coming at seven. The other girls didn't seem to be in any big rush, though. They were just lounging around, reading magazines.

"We've been planning this night for so long and now

it's finally arrived and we're totally unprepared," Min said.

"I'm prepared," Olivia announced, pulling a long strip of condoms out of her Hello Kitty pencil case.

"You have the condoms; you just don't have a date," Zola said, flipping through her magazine.

"Hey, that's not true," Olivia countered. "Bill's my date."

"I don't think it counts as dating if you've never once seen him off school grounds," Zola scoffed. She was stretched out on Min's bed in only her camouflage print bra and panties. Min stared at Zola's legs, which were long and toned. Zola was so lucky.

Olivia was watching Zola, too. She really wanted to start getting ready. They didn't have much time, and her hair was going to take at least a half hour. She wanted to put it up in a French twist, with the ends poking out. A tamed-tousled look. But Zola was being so blasé about everything, it would be lame of Olivia to act all hyper about getting dressed, even though she'd been planning her prom look for weeks.

"This all feels like nothing," Olivia said, trying to sound as casual as Zola. "It doesn't even feel like it's prom night and it's really happening."

"Too much buildup," Min said.

"This whole thing is for losers," Zola said, rolling over and turning the pages of her magazine with a stony expression.

Sally was trying to figure out why Zola was so upset.

She wondered if it had to do with her mother. Maybe Zola was sad that her mother couldn't be there to see her on the night of her senior prom. Zola pretended not to care about that kind of stuff, but Sally didn't believe it for a minute.

Sally took her new backless bra out of a shopping bag. They'd each bought one, even though Min was the only one going strapless. "How does this thing work?" she asked. She studied the bra, trying to make sense of all the weirdly crossed straps. Then she put it on over her T-shirt and pulled at the straps until they crossed her lower back and wrapped around her stomach. She tried to buckle it just above her belly button, but it kept flying open. "That scares me," she said, and tossed it on the floor.

Zola grabbed the bra off the floor and wrapped it around her head like some new trendy hair accessory. Olivia thought it actually looked good on her. Of course it did. Zola always looked good.

"I heard in LA the girls just wear a little duct tape over their nipples. Why don't you just use a little bit of duct tape, Sally?" Min said with a straight face. "I'll get my mom's craft basket."

"If there's ever a point in my life when I possess a craft basket, or anything even remotely craft related, promise me that one of you will just shoot me in the head and put me out of my craft-hell misery," Zola said.

"We promise," Olivia said.

"Come on, guys. We're running out of time. I'll go get some towels," Min said. She started undressing as she headed out the door, dropping her jeans and waddling out to the linen closet with them around her ankles. Ugh, Min thought, looking down at her thighs. After the prom there was going to be a party at Jason Altman's lake house. Min was only five-one and a tiny bit overweight. She wasn't really looking forward to wearing a bathing suit in front of the whole school.

Olivia opened *Cosmo* magazine and started reading about unwanted body hair removal. "Some people use a beard trimmer down there," she said, looking up from the magazine and giggling.

Min dropped a pile of fluffy pink towels on her bed and grabbed the magazine away from Olivia. "*Cosmo* likes the look of a narrow landing strip," she read out loud. "Landing strip! Hey, if we're going to wear our new suits tonight, we better depilitate," she said. She didn't want to be fat *and* hairy, thank you very much.

"I'm already depilitated," Zola announced. "I'm as smooth and hairless as a . . . What are those hairless cats called?"

"Which method did you use?" Min asked, holding up the magazine so Zola could see it.

"I got a bikini wax," Zola said. "I went to the Bare Facts Salon and got the Brazilian."

"Zola! How come you didn't tell me?" Olivia whined.

She'd *always* wanted to get a Brazilian wax, but she'd never had the guts. Now Zola had gone ahead and done it on her own.

"Do I have to tell you everything?" Zola complained.

"I just can't believe you didn't take me with you," Olivia said, pouting like a little kid.

"The Brazilian," Min said, intrigued.

"Yeah, and the next time I endure that much pain I better have some serious body art to show for it. When I got there a woman named Jonna asked if I wanted the Brazilian, the Penthouse, or the Happy Housewife."

"That's obscene!" Min crowed.

"And you chose the Brazilian?" Olivia asked.

"Well, it sounds a lot better than the Happy Housewife," Min said.

"And God only knows what the Penthouse entails," Zola said.

"Did it really hurt?" Sally asked.

"No, Sally, it didn't hurt at all. A crazy Polish woman puts hot wax on the most sensitive part of your body and then rips the hair out of you from the roots with strips of cloth as you scream and she makes small talk about the weather."

"Do you have a doll from Brazil?" Sally asked Min.

"I think so. She's the suntanned one in the peasant skirt and blouse behind the American Indian with the braids and the papoose."

Sally picked up the doll and turned it over. It was wearing long white cotton pantaloons. She tried to pull them down but they were sewn on.

Min snatched the doll out of Sally's hands. "Leave her alone, you pervert!" she said, and put the doll back on the shelf.

"Well, Zola shouldn't be the only one with a perfect bikini line. I'm going to shave mine," Olivia said. She knew she'd have razor burn tomorrow, but it was worth it for the prom.

She opened the door to the bathroom that adjoined Min's bedroom and ran the shower.

"I don't have any shaving cream," Min called.

"That's okay, I can use soap," Olivia said.

"I don't want to shave mine," Sally said timidly.

"Girl, if you're ever going to get a real date you're going to have to keep it neat and tidy down there. You'll thank me, I'm telling you," Zola said.

"I'm not shaving," Sally insisted. "And I do have a real date." She was going to the prom with Dean Merren, the cutest boy in her drama class.

"Well, if you don't want to shave I think I have an old bottle of Nair in here somewhere," Min said. She opened the cabinet under her bathroom sink and started rummaging. Min hated the smell of Nair. Kind of like farts and chemicals and dirty underwear mixed together. Once at camp, her bunk mates had all applied Nair to their legs and then sat out by the lake in the rain, letting the smelly cream run off their legs. But then it stopped raining and they didn't have time to shower, and at dinner the boys said, "What's that smell?" while making exaggerated sniffing sounds. It was really disgusting. That was the same summer she applied Jolen mustache bleach to the hair on her arms and a week later the hairs were half black and half blond. She had to wear long sleeves for the rest of the summer. "Here it is," she said, producing the pink bottle. "And here are some Daisy razors."

"Why do they make everything that has to do with girls pink?" Olivia asked.

"That's just one of the great mysteries of the universe," Zola said sarcastically. "Like is there a God, and what is our purpose here on Earth."

Olivia had thought she sounded cool and feminist pointing out the pink thing, but now she regretted saying it. Even though Olivia had the highest GPA of all of them and the third highest in the senior class—topped only by Claudia Choney and Olivia's sort-of boyfriend, Biology Bill Buchanan—Zola had a way of always making her observations sound dumb and trivial.

Min handed the Nair to Sally, and Sally stared at the bottle like it was some risky new drug she couldn't decide if she was bold enough to try.

"Go on, Sally," Zola said. "You know you want to."

There was a knock on Min's bedroom door. "Ladies, I can't wait to see you," Min's mother called through the door.

"Uh, there's not much to see yet, Mom," Min said. They were all still in their underwear.

Olivia opened the door to find Mrs. Weinstock standing there with a pitcher of iced tea and four glasses on a tray. It was hard to imagine Mrs. Weinstock with even the Happy Housewife. She looked like Martha Stewart with a more pronounced nose and chin, wearing capri chinos with a white sleeveless blouse tucked in, a slim pink belt, and a perfectly highlighted blond bob. She was the complete opposite of Olivia's mom, who dressed more like the doll from India, in long flowing clothes, and smelled like pot.

"Girls," she said, setting down the tray. "For some reason Mr. Otis from the school is sitting in my living room. He says he's here to pick up Zola."

Zola sat up straight on the bed, her 34Bs bouncing, and grabbed her dress out of her bag. "I'll be right down, Mrs. Weinstock," she said, blushing.

④

(Five-alarm Fire)

Min's mother closed the door and Min stared at Zola with her mouth open. Zola was full of surprises today. First the Brazilian and now this? Otis was the old guy who maintained the athletic equipment in the school gym. He was about a hundred years old and everybody loved him, but take him to the prom? He was a *maintenance man,* for Christ's sake. Zola, the coolest girl in the school, and possibly the world, was bringing an old geezer who was definitely wearing some sort of plaid flannel somewhere on his body to the fucking prom. Hello?

"Old man Otis is your date?" Min asked. "That's who you got the Brazilian for?"

"I asked him as a joke," Zola said vaguely. "I didn't think he'd actually show up."

"You asked *him?*" Olivia demanded.

"I told Evan I wasn't going with him and he said, "Oh yeah? Who are you going with, then?" We were in PE,

21

and Otis just looked so cute running around picking up the basketballs. So I walked right up to him and asked him to be my date for the prom. I really didn't think he'd show. But why not? I like older men."

"You have a father figure complex," Olivia said.

"Mrs. Zola Otis," Min said.

"I don't think Otis is his last name but it has a nice ring to it, anyway." Zola laughed.

"But you're kidding, right?" Min said. "I mean you are really going with Evan."

"Actually, I'm not kidding. I need a break from Evan and this whole prom thing. He was trying to make such a big production out of it and I finally told him it was becoming a huge turnoff. We ended up having a fight."

"I think it's nice that Evan wants to make a big deal out of it," Olivia said. She was worried. She happened to know Evan was still seriously into the prom thing and didn't believe for one minute that Zola was actually going with Otis. He had stopped Olivia in the hall at school last week and asked her what Zola's favorite flower was. She had told Evan she didn't think Zola liked any kind of flower; she only liked horses. "Well, she can't wear a horse on her wrist," Evan had said. Olivia had felt a little bit sorry for Evan.

"He really cares about you, Zola," Olivia added, hoping to encourage Zola to come to her senses.

"I know. He wrote a song called 'Zola' about going to the prom with me and then he played it for me Thursday night."

"See? That's so romantic," Olivia said enthusiastically.

"It *sounds* romantic, I guess," Zola said. "But for some reason it wasn't. I mean was I just supposed to sit there on his bed like a boring girlfriend and listen while he sang? My mind kept wandering, so I wasn't even listening to the song, and he kept asking me if I liked it, and I didn't know what to say. I kept thinking that it could have been any girl sitting there. It was almost like he wasn't really seeing me even though he was looking right at me and the girl in the song looked like me and was wearing this dress."

Actually, it *had* been romantic. It had been so romantic, it made Zola want to cry. But she would never tell anyone that.

"I don't understand, Zo. You've got a great-looking guy writing songs about you and you would rather go to the prom with old man Otis," Min said.

"I think I should write a song about a girl who badly needs therapy," Olivia said.

"I guess it is a little mean of me," Zola said. "You should have seen the look on Evan's face when I told him I was going with another boy."

"Boy!" Min shrieked. "I love the fact that you call old man Otis another *boy*."

Suddenly there was a yelp from behind the closed bathroom door. "Guys," Sally called. "Is this supposed to burn?"

"Tissue it off!" Min yelled.

"Ow, it *burns*."

"Run a cold tub, Sally," Zola ordered.

Sally looked in the mirror and started to cry. This was horrible. She didn't have the Brazilian or the Penthouse. She had the Five-Alarm Fire.

She had been writing in her diary while she waited for the Nair to kick in and now she picked up the pen again and wrote, *Right at this moment I am in serious pain. Note to self: Nair stinks!*

Sally blew out a trembling, frustrated sob. There was no way Dean was going to get anywhere near her bikini line, anyway. She didn't even know if it was a real date even though she was pretending it was. It was like Dean had been playing a part when he asked her. Dean was the best actor in the school and he was very serious about the method. Once, in drama class, they had practiced a sense memory exercise together. They had to pretend to do something and remember what it looked like, smelled like, felt like, tasted like. They had pretended to eat a wedge of lemon. Dean had made his left eye twitch and his lips purse. She thought he was winking at her but he was just reacting to the pretend lemon.

He looked so cute licking the imaginary lemon juice off his perfect lips.

Tonight she wanted to do a sense memory exercise of sex with Dean. They could pretend to put on an invisible condom and have invisible sex. But she wouldn't be very convincing. She had nothing to draw on. She didn't know how sex smelled, felt, or tasted. Every time she even thought about sex it was like running into a gigantic wall with her hands tied behind her back and her feet stuck in quicksand. She just froze up. It terrified her. Which is why she'd probably never be a great writer. Sally had seen *Shakespeare in Love*. She knew all great writers were great lovers. But now, in a matter of minutes, Dean was going to be picking her up for the prom, probably expecting to get lucky with the only female virgin left in the La Follette senior class, and all Sally could do was stand in front of the mirror, holding a cold washcloth between her legs, crying like a baby.

"All right, Sal, I'm coming in," Zola said. She opened the bathroom door, looking stunning in a demure black vintage dress. Very Audrey Hepburn in *Breakfast at Tiffany's*. Sally looked so pathetic wrapped in a fluffy pink towel, clutching her diary, with her legs spread wide apart. Zola felt like a superhero coming to the rescue.

Zola grabbed Sally's hand and led her to the foot of Min's bed. "Sit," she said. "I'm going to give you a makeover while you let your crotch air." She pulled Min's desk chair up to the bed and opened her makeup case. Sally was so cute with her baby-fine strawberry blond hair and blue eyes. She looked like she was about twelve years old.

"I don't suppose you'd let me tweeze those brows?" Zola asked.

"Nothing could be as bad as what I've already been through," Sally said bravely. She really wanted to look good for Dean. Zola grasped the pink tweezers in her hand and began to pluck. Sally squeezed her eyes shut and held her breath. It would all be over soon, and she could put on her dress and look like a princess.

"Well, it sounds like Evan's going stag to the prom, Sally. Maybe the two of you could hook up and he could write a song about your bald bikini line," Min joked.

"Yeah, he can sing it to everyone at the prom," Zola said. She tilted Sally's head and started working on the other eyebrow. A tear ran down Sally's cheek and Zola wiped it away with her thumb.

Olivia zipped Min up in her brown satin strapless gown. It was short in the front and brushed the floor in the back, very elegant with just a touch of Latin Explosion. It almost made her look tall. She had meant to wear something strappy and spangled but once she'd put this one on she couldn't imagine herself in anything else.

Olivia wore a tight crocheted Anna Sui sheath in light green. It was very retro chic with a touch of "did you make that yourself?" Her parents said if she got over 1300 on the SATs she could choose any dress she wanted. As soon as she opened the envelope with her results she went to them and said, "How high does my score have to be?"

"Thirteen hundred," her father said, smiling.

"That's awfully high," she said.

"Not for you," her mother said.

Olivia waved the envelope at them. "I don't know; thirteen hundred is a lot to ask."

Her father stood up and chased her around the room until he managed to get the envelope out of her hands. He pulled out the slip of paper. "Fifteen-twenty. Fifteen-twenty!" he said excitedly.

"Don't tell anyone," Olivia said.

"Not even Grandma?"

"I don't care about Grandma. Don't tell my friends. I don't want Min, Zola, and Sally knowing."

"Why not?" her father asked, looking baffled as usual.

"I just don't," she said firmly.

Sally's crotch was still burning, but it was time to get dressed. She tried to squirm out of Zola's grasp.

"Wait," Zola said, plucking one more hair from the right brow. "There," she said finally. "All done."

Sally looked in the mirror of Zola's compact. Now her bikini line wasn't the only thing red and swollen. Her eyebrows were pink and puffy and practically all gone.

"It looks good," Min said, walking up behind her. "Don't worry, the redness will fade in a minute."

Sally didn't believe her, but she forced herself to close the compact and move on. She unzipped the garment bag and a giant pink cloud blew out like a cotton candy explosion at a fair. She had found the most wonderful pink dress. It was straight out of *Guys and Dolls*. She couldn't wait to put it on.

Zola thought Sally's dress was insane. The puffs on her sleeves were bigger than her head and the dress actually had crinolines. Zola poked at one of the pink puffy sleeves and Min shot her a look to warn her against hurting Sally's feelings.

Min zipped Sally up. "You look beautiful," she told her. "Are we ready?" She stood back and admired her friends. Zola looked like a sixties film noir actress in her black dress and pearls. Olivia looked like she should be presenting the E! fashion awards. Sally's dress was silly, but she looked like she actually felt pretty in it.

"You all look amazing," Min said. "Come on. Let's go."

(5)

(Two Weeks to Graduation!)

"Well, hello, Otis," Zola said, walking into the Weinstocks' living room with Olivia, Min, and Sally right behind her. On her way downstairs she had decided to be polite and treat Otis like a real date. After all, he had insisted on picking her up. Now everyone at school would think she was an even bigger weirdo than they already did. It might be kind of fun.

"Heh, lo, oh," Otis said, standing awkwardly. He was wearing a tuxedo and his snow-white hair, or at least what there was left of it, was slicked straight back. He grabbed a bouquet of red roses from the coffee table and handed them to Zola.

"Thank you, Otis; that's so sweet," she said, taking the roses and kissing him on the cheek. He smelled like Colgate shaving cream and reminded Zola of her grandfather, Oppa Zeke, who lived in Seattle.

"You look very beautiful, Zola," Otis said, blushing.

"And you look very handsome, Otis. I don't think I've ever seen you in anything but flannel."

Otis opened his tuxedo jacket and pulled the waistband of his plaid flannel boxer shorts up so the girls could see that he was in fact wearing flannel.

"Hello, girls," a voice said behind them.

It was Rabbi Weinstock, home from teaching a course at the university.

"Hello, sir, your honor, sir," Otis said, buttoning his tux.

"Hello, Otis. I've told you a million times, call me Steve," Rabbi Weinstock said. Min had played girls' soccer for three years and he had met Otis many times. The rabbi pulled off his tie and reached out to shake Otis's hand. "So, are you chaperoning tonight, Otis?"

Zola stepped forward. "Otis is escorting me to the prom," she said levelly.

Mr. Weinstock raised his eyebrows, but he didn't say anything. He had known Min's friends all their lives. They were so full of surprises that nothing they did could shock him anymore.

"I was just showing the girls that I was still wearing flannel," Otis said. "Finest quality."

Rabbi Weinstock laughed. "Let me see my beautiful daughter," he said, admiring Min in her gown. "Watch out!" he shouted, his eyes shining. "She's *smoking!*" He stood back and admired Olivia, Sally, and Zola. "Oh, we're going to break some hearts tonight!" he said, and winked at Otis. "Hold on, I'd better get my camera." He dashed upstairs, shouting for Mrs. Weinstock as he went.

"Min, your phone's ringing," Min's mother called from the top of the stairs.

Min ran as fast as she could in her gown and heels, but when she got to her room the machine had picked up. Tobias was leaving a message.

"Hey, I can't pick you up. We're going to have to meet you there," he said. Then he broke into puppy talk. "Because somwuff's not feewing vewy wuff and we've been soooo worried. Ozzy, don't eat that, good boy. My poor Ozzy." The dial tone sounded.

Min noticed the answering machine was flashing the number two. There was another message.

"Hello. This is a message for Sally. It's Dean. Ah, I'm running a little late, working out a rough patch in this monologue I'm working on. I think I'm really close to something here and I don't want to stop. So, I'll meet you at the prom, okay? By the water fountain at say, eight-fifteen. All right? Thanks. See you there. Bye."

Min returned to the living room to find Otis grooving with Zola, Olivia, Sally, and both of her parents to a Lauryn Hill CD. Her mother and father loved to dance and they both had great rhythm, but it was pretty embarrassing. Otis held his hands in fists and shuffled his feet. It looked like he was holding himself back from really cutting loose.

"Tobias can't pick me up," Min told them. "And Dean isn't coming, either. They said they'll meet us there." Min was disappointed. It's not that she expected the whole limo thing, but she might have liked to have a picture of herself heading off to the prom with her boyfriend. Her father had the camera all ready to go, hanging from a strap around his neck.

"I have my truck," Otis offered. "Of course two of you girls will have to ride in the back."

Rabbi Weinstock walked over to the window and pulled back the curtain. He looked out at the open-bed truck with the La Follette Ferrets bumper sticker and the Garfield doll suction cupped to the window.

"You can take the Subaru," he said. He turned and raised the camera to his face. "Okay, everyone say, 'Two weeks to graduation!'"

Zola wrapped one arm around Otis's thick waist and the other arm around Sally's shoulders.

Sally blinked at the flash and turned red. She hated having her picture taken, but she knew she'd treasure these pictures when she was older. She'd paste them in her diary after the part where she'd written all about the prom. She was nervous about meeting Dean, so she didn't really mind that he was meeting her there. She couldn't wait to see what would happen. Most of all, she couldn't wait to write about it.

(6)

(Motherless Angel)

Otis followed in his truck as Min pulled out of the drive-way in her father's car, or the Mitzvah Mobile, as she liked to call it, because her father had been the rabbi in attendance at hundreds and hundreds of bar mitzvahs. Just then a black stretch limousine pulled in. The chauffeur got out and walked around to the back and opened the door. Evan Fell, dressed in a top-of-the-line rented tux that he had chosen to match the tux Matt Damon wore to the Oscars because he remembered Zola saying she liked it, stepped out onto the Weinstocks' gravel.

He bent down to take one last look inside the limo. He wanted everything to be perfect. He had a bottle of champagne chilling in a bucket of ice. There were two champagne glasses with little paper napkins wrapped around them printed with a picture of a couple kissing in silhouette. He knew the limo and the napkins were tacky, but he also knew Zola loved that kind of thing. The more

33

over-the-top the better. She always asked for umbrellas and pineapple slices in her drink, even if she was only having a Coke. And her favorite restaurant in town was Stewart's, a fifties throwback where you turn your car lights on and the carhop takes your order and brings your burgers and root beer floats right to the car on a little tray that balances in the window. Zola was cool enough to see the beauty in tacky things, although she was the most untacky girl in the world.

Evan gingerly picked up the corsage in its crinkly plastic box. The man in the flower store had instructed him to keep it in his refrigerator all day and Evan had taken endless abuse about it from his younger brother, Todd. Todd had aped with it all day, tossing it around, putting a Post-it on it that said, *To Zola from your favorite loser,* and hiding it behind jars of Hellmann's and Grey Poupon.

Evan had discussed the corsage at great length with Brendan, the owner of Brendan's Floral Fantasy. Evan had told Brendan that Zola's dress was black.

"Black? Who wears black to the prom?" Brendan had asked, with his hands pressed together in front of his chest as if he were praying.

"I don't know; I guess she just likes being different," Evan told him.

"And is it silk taffeta?" Brendan asked, getting slightly wistful. "I just love taffeta."

"I think so," Evan said, even though he had no idea.

Brendan gasped. "Divine," he said.

"It's sort of old," Evan told him.

"Old! You mean it's used? She got a Salvation Army special?" Brendan sneered. "Maybe we'll go with Gerber daisies."

"No, it's more antiquey," Evan said, getting flustered.

"Oh, it's *vintage,*" Brendan said. "Fabulous. What era? Nineteen-twenties? Thirties? Forties? Oh, I hope it's the forties."

"I'm not sure. It belonged to her mother. Her mother's dead."

"That's just tragic," Brendan said. "I'm going to design the most beautiful corsage that ever came out of Madison for your motherless angel. It will be tiny fragrant purple roses with sprigs of lily of the valley to be worn on the wrist. But I'll leave room for artistic license in case something comes to me."

Brendan had been right. The corsage was beautiful. Evan had opened the refrigerator door about a hundred times that day just to take it out and look at it for a moment. Zola had been acting like she didn't even want to go to the prom and even pretended to ask old man Otis to be her date, but Evan was sure she was just nervous about the future. They were so close to graduation, and who knew what would happen next. But Evan wasn't nervous. That night he was going to tell Zola that he loved her. And to show her how he felt he was going to try to keep his pants on and concentrate on her. After that, it would be different. She wouldn't be nervous anymore. She would know he wanted them to stay together forever.

"I hope your girlfriend's *here*," the chauffeur said. "I hope we're not going to have to drive all over town looking for her."

Evan gave him a dirty look. He wasn't paying all this money for attitude. They had gone to Zola's house first but she wasn't there. Her father said she was getting ready at Min's.

"She's here," Evan said.

He went up to the front door and rang the bell. Rabbi Weinstock answered.

"Uh, hello, sir, Father, Mr. . . . ," Evan stuttered.

"It's Steve," Rabbi Weinstock said.

"I'm here to pick up Zola for the prom."

"They just left," Rabbi Weinstock said. He peered at the limo parked outside. Why couldn't Min date a nice young man like this one instead of Tobias? "Perhaps there was a misunderstanding?" Rabbi Weinstock said.

"Yeah, I'm sure there was," Evan said. His face felt hot and he wanted to rip off his stupid black tuxedo tie. "Sorry to bother you." He turned in his slippery black shoes and took the long walk of shame back to the car. The driver shook his head at him and looked impatiently at his watch. Evan wanted to punch him. He had never felt like this before. Like his insides had been run over by a train, and Zola was the conductor. He got back into the limo and downed a minibottle of Dewar's.

"Just take me to the damn prom," he told the driver.

(Skank)

Min pulled up in the school's parking lot and Olivia and Zola got out of the car.

"Okay, Sally, we're here," Min said.

Sally was writing in her diary on her lap. *So this is it. The day I never thought would come. I feel numb. I have to try to feel what it feels like to be at my senior prom. Soon I will be dancing with Dean Merren and looking into his eyes. I think I will definitely kiss him.*

"Sally?" Min repeated.

Sally looked up. "Oh, sorry," she said. She closed the book and shoved it in her backpack, which was red and totally clashed with her dress.

"You're going to drag that thing around?" Zola asked.

Sally nodded. Zola knew she never went anywhere without her diary. And the only thing she had to carry it in was her backpack.

The parking lot was packed with cars, and kids were

milling about in their prom gear, posing for pictures and shouting and drinking in their cars. Olivia stopped to check out what people were wearing. Deidre Bates, the class vice president, had on the exact same lavender dress that Olivia had tried on at Neiman Marcus four times before deciding it was too boring. What a relief she hadn't bought it. Deidre was tall and flat and too thin for the dress, which gaped under her arms so much you could see her nipples. Olivia felt embarrassed for her. Rich Jackson, the saxophone player, had grown out his red sideburns and was wearing a neon green frilly tux shirt, open at the collar, with a fat gold chain around his neck. His tight black pants accentuated his hips, which were wide like a girl's. Rich was carrying a huge plastic jug of vodka and offering it to everyone he saw, trying to make friends. He probably thought he looked like a rock star but he really looked like an idiot. Once in sixth grade Rich had told Olivia that she could be pretty if she didn't open her mouth, and Olivia had hated him ever since.

The high school actually looked kind of cool, Min had to admit. There were lights crisscrossing the sky, so it suddenly felt more exciting, more like a Hollywood movie premiere than the same old boring La Follette High prom. Min looked around for Tobias's Jeep but it wasn't there yet. Tobias had been giving her grief all week about having to go to the prom. "But Minnie Mouse, I did all this already when *I* graduated," he said. "It's going to be exactly the same."

Min couldn't argue with that. For some inane reason the La Follette High senior prom had had the same theme for four years—the *Titanic*. Every year the gym was decorated like the famous ship and the sound track from the movie was played over and over. Some of the teachers dressed in sailor suits or like rich tycoons. It was one of those things people thought worked well enough to turn into a tradition, like eating turkey on Thanksgiving or throwing your bouquet at your wedding. Min thought it was the worst idea anyone had ever had, but she still wanted to come to the prom, and she wanted Tobias there, too. She hoped he'd show up soon.

"You know, I think we're actually going to have a really good time," Zola said, surprising herself. Without Evan, she felt vulnerable and dangerous at the same time, as though she could do anything she wanted to. Otis slammed the door to his pickup and shuffled toward her. Zola was going to be nice to him and dance with him, but after a little while she knew Otis would be off fixing a leaky pipe or something, and she'd be free to do what she pleased. The first thing she was going to do was find Evan.

"Hi, girlfriends," a voice said behind them.

They turned to see Claudia Choney approaching in an obscene electric blue strapless gown. Her chest looked like it had doubled in size since Friday at three o'clock. Scott Stewart, the captain of the football team, was right beside her, holding out his arm in case she fell off her platforms.

"Hi, Claudia," Zola said. Little Miss Sickening Sweater Set actually looked pretty hot.

"Looking good, girls," Claudia said. She tried to smile, but whenever Claudia smiled it came out as a sneer. "Where are your dates?"

Just then old man Otis came up behind Zola, holding a giant plunger. "I thought I better bring this in from the truck. Keep it nice 'n' handy for when the toilets get blocked up in the ladies' room. Happens every darn year," he said. "May I escort my lovely date into the prom?" he asked sweetly, holding his arm out to Zola.

Claudia Choney gasped. "Where's Evan?"

Zola shrugged.

"Really! I'll have to remember to grab a dance with him. If that's okay?" Claudia said.

"It's a free country," Zola answered. Suddenly she didn't want to make a big deal out of walking in with Otis. Claudia had sort of ruined it for her. All she wanted to do was find Evan and tell him she was sorry. In fact, she was already sorry she hadn't just let him pick her up at Min's. She turned to Otis. "I'll meet you in there, okay?" she said.

"Okeydokey," Otis said. He winked at her, reminding

41

Zola of Santa Claus, and shuffled off toward the school entrance, carrying his plunger.

Scott took Claudia's hand. "Wow, Zola, you look amazing," he said. "That's probably going to be the coolest dress at the whole prom. Doesn't she look great, Cloudy?"

Zola could practically see Claudia's hackles rise at her date's question. "See you in there," she snarled at the girls, dragging Scott away.

"What a skank," Sally said, surprising herself. She had never said the word *skank* before and she wanted to make a note to herself to use it a lot from now on. "If I ever write a book I'm going have a Claudia character and call her Skank."

Zola laughed. You didn't really expect something like that to come out of Sally's mouth.

"Skank what? What would her last name be?" Olivia asked.

"Maybe Skank McPherson," Sally said.

"I love you, Sally," Zola said, wiping tears of laughter out of her eyes. Sally was the only one who could really make her laugh.

"I think Claudia has a thing for Evan," Olivia remarked. "A big thing."

"No, she's just being a bitch," Zola insisted.

"Well, I don't know; I think she's in love with him."

"He would never go for her," Zola said confidently. Evan didn't even know Claudia existed. "Her boobs are too—"

Suddenly the deafening sound of a motorcycle drowned out the end of her sentence. A man on a shiny black motorcycle, wearing a white leather jacket, waved as he sped by.

"Look, it's the Fonz," Min said, pointing.

"No, he looks like Lenny Kravitz," Sally said.

"You're just obsessed with Lenny Kravitz," Min said. It was sort of true. Sally had a poster of him in her room. She had found it on a bench in the mall and liked it for some reason. There was just something about him. She didn't know it was Lenny Kravitz until Olivia came over one day and asked her why she had a poster of him over her bed.

"But that guy really does look like him," Olivia said. "I could have sworn that *was* Lenny Kravitz."

"Guys, are we going to spend the whole prom in the parking lot?" Zola asked. She tugged on Sally's back-pack. "Come on. Let's go in."

Side by side, they paraded toward the gym door as if they were walking on a red carpet instead of the cigarette-stubby school parking lot. Before they went inside, Sally took one last look around for the motorcycle-riding stranger, but he was gone.

Clarence sped along the main road behind the school until he smelled water. Then he turned down a dirt road and took it all the way to the end, until he came to the shore of Lake Waubesa. The water stretched out before him, deep and black, lapping listlessly against the pebbly beach. Clarence parked his bike and opened a minibottle of champagne, which he'd taken from one of the empty limos in the school parking lot. He sipped the champagne and looked at the placid lake, breathing deeply. Water was so relaxing. Clarence realized he'd been under so much pressure lately he'd forgotten to take any time for himself to enjoy Earth's pleasures. A little downtime was exactly what he needed.

It had been his plan to introduce himself to the girls *before* the prom. After all, he was on a mission, and he wanted to get started right away. But when he saw Min, Sally, Zola, and Olivia, all dressed up, with this wonderful look of expectation on their faces, he couldn't bring himself to do it. Especially Sally. How could he show her her future before she'd even been to her own prom, knowing she'd be back again and again, time immemorial? Sure, some of the news he had to deliver wasn't the happiest, but Clarence wasn't cruel. He was no Ghost of Christmas Past, scaring the wits out of people. He wanted the girls to like him.

So Clarence had decided to wait. He finished the bottle of champagne and sat down on the shore in lotus position and began to meditate, stepping out of the stressful job of being a fairy godmother and into quiet space of his mind, radiating peace and well-being to all living things. Clarence had just finished a book called *The Buddha at Work*. The book said that all meditation has the same goal: to help know yourself more deeply, and by knowing yourself, to know others as well. When the time came to reach out to the girls, he would *know*. Simple as that.

He sure hoped it would be sooner rather than later, though. He'd been practicing yoga for aeons, but sitting on the pebbly ground was seriously uncomfortable, especially in knee-high leather boots.

8

(Our Hearts Will Go On)

Olivia walked past a group of teachers dressed in blue-and-white ship's captain costumes, swaying to the music. The gym was strung with ropes and lifeboats and painted foam life preservers that read HMS *La Follette*. There were imitation Persian rugs and seaweed on the floor. The decorating committee had really gone all out with the *Titanic* theme this year. Someone had even taped a sign on the girls' bathroom door that said the Head. Olivia knew that was the nautical term for toilet, but it didn't seem to make any sense in the high school gym. Up on-stage, The Stormy Knights were warming up with Elton John's "Crocodile Rock." As usual, Olivia thought, the prom was going to suck.

"This seaweed shit rocks!" Zola exclaimed, kicking a clump of it into the air. Olivia watched as Zola pulled Otis onto the dance floor and started to do the twist, getting as low to the floor as possible, almost like she was squatting

46

for a pee. Zola looked like she was determined to have a good time, Olivia thought.

Maybe the prom wouldn't suck. Maybe something would happen to surprise everyone.

Bill stood near the punch, talking to the other members of the biology club. Olivia went up and tapped him on the shoulder.

"Hi," she said.

"Hi," he said back.

"And we thought they didn't have deep conversations," Olivia heard Zola say behind her. She turned around and glared at her friend.

"Do you want to dance?" Olivia asked Bill.

Bill shook his head. "I told you I hate dancing."

"Come on, Bill. It's the prom."

"Really?" he said.

Olivia put her hands on her hips. "I just thought we could try to talk and dance and have a good time for once."

"We always have a good time," he said. He took her hand and led her to the dance floor. Olivia thought he was going to be romantic. They were going to dance. But then he led her across the dance floor. And off the dance floor. And right out of the gym and upstairs to the biology lab. "I like being alone with you," he said.

It was true. He wasn't just being sleazy. Bill hated

being around crowds of people and he couldn't imagine why Olivia would want to be downstairs at that suck fest instead of all alone with him.

She looked great in her cool green dress, but she looked better naked. He started kissing her neck. Then he picked her up and put her on the lab table between two Bunsen burners, continuing to kiss her.

For a science nerd Bill wasn't such a bad kisser. In fact, Olivia thought he was a kind of great kisser.

She ran her fingers through his soft brown hair and opened her eyes so she could look at his eyelashes but for some reason she couldn't get into it. She could hear the Celine Dion song coming on and girls were screaming. There were all those couples downstairs dancing together—why weren't they with them? Olivia liked Bill but practically their entire relationship had taken place in the bio lab storage closet. It would be nice to have sex without it turning into a ménage à trois with the life-size hanging human skeleton who Bill referred to as Red Skeleton, after some old dead comedian.

Bill went to get a condom from his private stash in the closet behind the boxes of slides. Then he unzipped his tux pants and lifted Olivia's dress up around her thighs. They had sex on the table while Olivia looked over Bill's shoulder at a wall chart of the glands of the human body. She liked biology, but she didn't think she would major in it in college. She wondered what college she would wind up going to. Was it dumb to turn down MIT? Absently, Olivia felt Bill run his hands down her back and press his face into her shoulder. Her back arched as her body responded, and it felt good, but her mind was far, far away. What's the matter with me? She wondered. There had to be more to love and sex than this. It was all biology and not enough chemistry.

"What's wrong?" Bill asked.

Olivia looked into his big brown eyes. He looked so cute with his tux pants pulled down and the little beads of sweat forming on his forehead. And he looked like he was really into it, like she was the hottest girl in the whole world. Suddenly Olivia didn't want to think about the future. She didn't want to think about anything. Instead she closed her eyes, wrapped her legs around Bill's waist, and pulled herself up against him to give physics a chance to work its magic.

⑨

(You're So Vain)

Sally found Dean in their appointed meeting spot at the water fountain. She was almost surprised to see him standing there. She wanted to write, *He's here!* in her diary.

"I'm really glad you decided to come to the prom with me," Dean said. He looked deeply into Sally's eyes. He made his eyeballs move back and forth from right to left as if he was looking into her eyes individually, one at a time, the way soap opera actors did. "I've really liked you for quite a while now."

"You have?" Sally asked.

"Yeah, I find you really interesting. I really loved your play." He smiled and pushed his blond hair back with his hand.

Sally cocked her head and tried to figure out if Dean was for real. There was no way to tell, he was such a good actor.

"Are you having a good time?" Dean asked, looking at Sally like she was a precious little girl.

"Yeah," she said.

"I really want you to have a good time. I want us always to remember this."

"I have a really good memory," Sally said. Jesus, that was stupid. Between the pounding beat of the interminable *Titanic* song and the punch and the rapid movement of Dean's eyeballs, she was starting to feel dizzy.

"I can tell that about you," Dean said. "That's one of the things I like about you."

"What?" Sally said.

"Your memory."

"I write everything down. I keep a diary," she said. Now things were going from bad to worse. I keep a diary. It made her sound like she was about twelve. Now Dean would realize she was completely and totally unfucked. Why didn't she just wear a T-shirt that said *geek* on the front and *virgin* on the back?

"I keep a diary, too," Dean said. "Well, not really a diary. It's more of a journal. As an actor, I find it very important to write a lot. I enjoy journaling. I try to journal as much as possible."

Until that moment Sally had always hated people who used *journal* as a verb.

"Wow, I can't believe we both journal," she said.

"Do you want to dance, Sally?" Dean asked.

Sally tried to pull herself together. "Okay," she mumbled.

Dean made a dramatic after-you gesture with his hands and she walked in front of him onto the dance floor. He put his hands around her waist and she swayed back and forth. Then he took her arms and put them around his neck and they danced that way for a minute or two. Sally could smell Dean's cologne. Her nose itched and she thought she might be allergic to it.

"Sally, I know this is going to sound lame," Dean said. "It's just that your opinion is very important to me. I was wondering if you would watch me do this monologue I've been working on. I really want it to be in good shape by the time I get to Tisch in September."

"Tisch?" Sally asked, confused.

"Sorry. That's what we call the acting department at NYU. New York University—Tisch School of the Arts. Tisch. Anyway, would you listen to my monologue?"

"Sure," Sally said, her arms still happily around his neck.

"Wow, that's so great. I can't wait to do it for you. I consider myself to be a very spontaneous person."

The band broke out into something incredibly loud and unrecognizable. It sounded like The Stormy Knights thought the *Titanic* theme was pretty lame, too, and they were rebelling.

"What?" Sally screamed.

"I'm a spontaneous person," Dean screamed back.

Sally just nodded.

"I'd love for you to hear the monologue but I don't want to bore you. You probably wouldn't like it."

"Yes, I would," Sally said.

"I don't want you to think I'm all full of myself or anything. You probably think I probably think this song is about me."

"Yes. I mean, no," Sally said. She looked up at Dean, completely confused. The next thing she knew he was leading her off the dance floor. She knew he wouldn't want to keep dancing with her. He probably wished he had brought someone else.

(Bad Boy!)

"Sally?" Min said, tugging on her friend's puffy pink sleeve. "Have you seen Tobias?"

Sally shook her head and kept walking. Min watched Dean lead her out the gym door to the back stairs and wondered where they were going. Maybe this was Sally's lucky night, she thought.

Tobias had just arrived, but he was in the bathroom with Ozzy. Min thought he was going to leave Ozzy home, but the poor dog had such bad diarrhea Tobias didn't want to leave him alone. He had even dressed Ozzy in a little black bow tie. Min crossed her arms over her stomach and leaned against the punch table. She felt stupid for getting all dressed up while her boyfriend spent the whole prom in the bathroom with his dog.

Just then Ozzy ran by with a piece of red licorice in his teeth. The licorice was longer than he was. Tobias was right behind him and dove to the floor, wrestling the licorice out of Ozzy's mouth. "Bad boy!" he said, stuffing it into his own mouth and chewing it up. He stole a sheepish look at Min. "Now, go tell Mommy how pretty she looks."

Min blushed and finished chewing the handful of pretzels she'd just stuffed into her mouth. Tobias looked so sexy, sprawled on that brown Persian rug, with strands of fake seaweed in his hair, she wanted to jump him. She took a swig of punch and sauntered up to him.

"Fancy a dance?" she asked, trying to sound like Kate Winslet in *Titanic*. "If you're any good I might let you draw naked pictures of me later."

Ozzy barked at her and Tobias pulled a little daisy out of his pocket. He stood up and put it in Min's hair. Min wrapped her arms around him and they kissed and Min didn't feel angry at Tobias anymore. She knew he would make it up to her; he always did.

(Chance)

Dean opened the heavy door to the auditorium and told Sally to sit in the center of the seventh row. He slid out the side door and appeared a moment later, onstage.

"Okay," he said. "Let me set it up for you. I'm a really great-looking guy named Chance and I'm sort of a gigolo and I'm staying in a hotel with this rich older woman. So picture me in just silk boxer shorts or something like that. Although I guess I could be wearing a tux; that would be an interesting choice." He paused for a moment, deep in thought. "No, I'm definitely wearing silk boxers. Red."

Dean started the monologue. "Really, Irene. Saying my penis is bigger than anyone else's is hardly a compliment. I've seen racehorses with smaller dicks. More wine? No? It's good. I didn't know they made such good wine in Oregon. And you really shouldn't talk about me to your friends. . . ."

He stopped. "Can you hear me?"

"Yes," Sally said. Sally sat in the seventh row, watching Dean's every move. She felt like she was hearing him with every part of her body, not just her ears.

"I just wanted to make sure I'm projecting."

He cleared his throat and continued the monologue. "And you really shouldn't talk about me to your friends. I know you don't mean anything, but it's bragging. And bragging can be a real turnoff, Irene, let me tell you. Here's a towel. Would you like me to put some lotion on your back? I bought you a bottle of Fracas lotion. It's Jean LaPorte, from Paris. Very expensive. It reminds me of my mother; she always wore Fracas. Oh God! Every time I see you I say I'm not going to do this again. Come here."

Dean stopped again. "You know, it's hard for me to move my body the way I have to in this tux. The character is very physical. Very sexual, actually. Do you mind if I try it in the costume? It really helps me to become Chance."

Sally knew she was blushing. She tried to give a casual shrug and Dean went offstage and came back again a moment later wearing nothing but his red silk boxer shorts and black socks. Sally couldn't stand it any longer. She pulled her diary out of her backpack, opened it on her lap, and began writing.

I'm sure he doesn't like me, she wrote. *I'm a terrible*

dancer. I was so nervous I was falling all over myself. But here he is doing a very sexual monologue wearing practically nothing. I wonder where he got the idea for his play. I wonder if he's actually had affairs with older women in hotel rooms. He would die if he knew I've only been kissed once in my whole entire life.

Her first and only kiss had been with a boy named David Braverman. Sally loved his last name, Braverman. He played the piano for the musical productions at camp. They took a field trip to see *Gypsy* at the Ogunquit Playhouse, and when they were getting on the bus to go back to the camp, he asked if he could sit next to her. He took the window seat and she slid in after him. He took off his glasses and leaned way in to her and kissed her and she felt his braces on her lips. But it was soft, too. After they kissed for a while they just sat in silence. And then he got sick. He threw up out of the bus window and sat for the rest of the trip with his jacket on his head.

(10)

(Motherless Angel, Part 2)

Zola couldn't find Evan. She felt strangely out of place without him and had looked everywhere, hoping to spot him. They had been practically inseparable for three and a half years and it just felt wrong to be wandering around the prom without him. And, despite the compliment from Scott, she felt weird in her mother's black dress. She looked so different from the other girls. She wished she had let Olivia talk her into buying a long strappy gown at Burdines.

And she wished she hadn't given Evan such a hard time. She had wanted to feel free to dance with other people but now she just felt stupid. Who was she supposed to dance with? Eric Lipp, who carried his T square around with him even if he didn't have to? Marcus Grossman, who got suspended for masturbating into his violin case in the library? Alaric Rael, who compulsively scratched his name into his skin with the point of his compass?

Evan hadn't even shown up. The feeling that something good was going to happen had definitely been left behind in the parking lot and been run over by a car. Zola suddenly felt like leaving, but she couldn't ask Min to drive her home. It wouldn't be fair. Min looked like she was having a good time, dancing with Tobias and Ozzy. Zola wished she still smoked so she would at least have a reason to go outside. She had quit smoking when her mother had to go through chemotherapy. Her mother's cancer wasn't smoking related but Zola just had to spend one day in the waiting room of the cancer pavilion and she'd instantly quit. She didn't say anything when her friends smoked, though. She hated people like that.

She decided to go outside, anyway, and breathed deeply when she got out to the parking lot. The lot was packed with cars and a few limos. A chauffeur, wearing a hokey cap, got out and leaned against his limo.

She wished she had just let Evan pick her up in a limo the way he wanted to. She had never even been in one.

The driver saw her looking his way and gave a little wave.

"Do you have a cigarette?" he called.

Zola couldn't hear what he said, so she walked over to him. He made a smoking motion with his hands.

"Oh, I don't smoke," she said.

"I saw you standing there, and I couldn't help but admire you in that dress," the chauffeur said.

"Oh, really," Zola said wryly.

"Well, of course. You're a very beautiful woman."

Zola had never been called a woman before by an older man. He had a thin brown mustache and was sort of handsome in a retro way.

"What's your name?" the chauffeur asked. "Lolita?"

Zola giggled and fingered her mother's pearls. "Close," she said. "It's Zola."

"Zola, don't tell me you're alone," the chauffeur said. "Your boyfriend's probably inside looking for you."

"Actually, he didn't show up." Zola sighed.

"There seems to be a lot of that going around," the driver said. He pointed to the limo. "The guy I drove here couldn't track down his date, either. But I guess he found another girl roaming around."

"Gross," Zola said, making a face.

"My name is Joe, by the way," the chauffeur said.

Zola sized him up. He looked so square and lonely and she felt so random without Evan. She'd wanted to run around the school with him, fooling around in unlikely places, peeing in the radiators. But Evan didn't even come. And Zola felt like she just had to do something wild and reckless, *right now,* or she would die.

"Don't you think it would be kind of a shame if I spent the whole night looking this good and I didn't kiss anyone?" Zola asked Joe. She took a step toward him.

"Yes, it would," Joe said. He smiled, waiting.

Now that she was closer, Zola could smell his cologne. Evan never wore cologne. She hadn't kissed anyone but Evan since freshman year. This was what she wanted, wasn't it? New experiences, other men, something new and exciting to happen?

She grabbed Joe's hand and opened the limo door with her free hand, pulling him in behind her. But Joe wriggled out of her grasp.

"Come on. I want to see what it's like inside one of these things," Zola told him.

She ducked her head inside the backseat and found herself face-to-face with Evan. And straddling his lap was Claudia Choney.

(11)

(Send Him to Me)

Sally was determined to be kissed that night. She wanted Dean to kiss her. So when he finished his monologue and suggested that they go out to his car where he'd stashed a bottle of Jägermeister, she said a very brave yes.

They sat in his car in the parking lot and he took a sip from the green bottle and offered it to her. The bottle looked like something old men would drink when they go ice fishing in a lodge somewhere. There was some sort of buck on it with antlers and a cross. She took a tiny sip. It was disgusting.

"Do you like Jägermeister?" he asked.

"Ummm, yes," she said. "I love Jägermeister."

"I like you, Sally," he said.

"I like you, too, Dean." It was finally happening. She adjusted her hand on her knee so Dean might notice it and try to hold it. She stretched her fingers for a second. Then she turned her hand over so her palm was facing up invitingly. She never knew she could be the kind of girl who sat in the car of a gorgeous boy and drank Jägermeister.

He shifted in the driver's seat and turned toward her. He leaned in to her as if he was about to kiss her. Sally closed her eyes. For a second nothing happened. Then she heard Dean make a strange choking sound. She opened her eyes to find Dean holding his face in his hands and shaking. She didn't know what was happening. Then she realized he was crying.

He was rocking back and forth, sniffing and wiping his eyes and nose with the sleeves of his tux. He looked like he was having a nervous breakdown.

"What's wrong?" Sally finally asked.

Dean didn't respond. He just kept rocking and sniffling. Sally had no idea what to do. She put her hand on the back of his head and started to stroke his short blond hair. It didn't even seem awkward. It felt natural to touch him in that comforting way. But Dean shrugged her hand away.

"No, don't touch me," he cried. "I don't want you to see me like this."

"Dean, tell me, what is the matter?"

He sniffled softly for a few seconds and then sobbed even harder, as if he'd suddenly thought of a reason to really feel sorry for himself. Sally looked out the window. Why was this happening? She wondered. God, she thought, as if she were writing in her journal, where is the boy I am supposed to meet? Where is he? Send him to me.

Finally Dean's sobs subsided. "It's just that this is the *prom,*" he said in a choked-up voice. "And then yearbooks and the last day of school, the last day of *high* school, and graduation and the summer. And then we're all going off in all our separate directions. I'll probably never see anyone again. I won't see you, the guys, or Mrs. Williams, or Ms. Sheinman. . . ."

Sally couldn't believe Dean was acting like this. He sounded like such a baby. It was hard to believe he'd just been doing a macho monologue about a gigolo.

"And I'll be at NYU, where anything could happen. I'll be with all new people, living in New York, for Christ's sake, and then I'll go to summer stock and I'll get an agent and go on auditions, and I'll have new girlfriends and maybe meet the woman I'm going to marry."

Was this supposed to be romantic? Sally wondered. Was a boy supposed to burst into tears and tell you that he was about to move to New York to meet the woman he was going to marry right before kissing you on prom night? Dean was acting like a jerk, and it was getting really annoying.

"I mean, what's going to happen to me?" Dean continued. "Am I going to be able to handle living in New York, I mean, come on, *New York City,* Jesus, and all I want is to be a good actor, I mean, I just want to go there and show them they did the right thing to accept me into the drama program and just get deep into the work. All I want is to do good work."

Sally had never seen such a self-centered idiot. What was she supposed to say? She wasn't exactly the school guidance counselor. What did he want her to do about it? "Your nose is running," she said.

"I'm sorry," he said. "I'm probably not showing you that great of a time." He started to cry again. Hard.

"Actually, it is kind of boring," Sally said. Immediately she felt guilty for sounding so cruel. "I mean it's the prom and we should be dancing or something. Everything will work out fine for you, Dean, I'm sure. You're a very gifted actor."

"Do you really think so?" Dean sniffed.

"Of course. You're going to NYU." She tried to say "NYU" as reverently as he did.

"Well, would you mind if I just sit here alone for a little while? I just really need to be alone," Dean said.

There goes my kiss, Sally thought. Just then she saw Zola practically running across the parking lot. She opened the window. "Zola," she yelled.

Zola turned around to see who was calling her and saw Sally waving from the front seat of the blue Honda. Zola walked over to her, happy to see her. "Sally, I'm so glad to see you," she said. She knew she sounded really upset, but she couldn't wipe the image of Evan and Claudia together in the limo out of her mind. "Hi, Dean," she said.

Dean wiped his nose on his sleeve. "Hi, Zola," he said in a husky voice.

"Hey, can I have some of that?" Zola asked. She reached into the car and took the bottle of Jägermeister. She took a big swig.

"What's wrong, Zola?" Sally asked.

"Nothing," Zola said, but her voice quavered. "I'm just mad. I should leave you guys alone." She winked at Sally. But Sally looked like she was eager to get out of there. Zola got the feeling she had come to Sally's rescue again.

"No, you're upset. I'll go with you," Sally said, opening the car door.

"Thanks, Sal. Hey, Dean, you don't mind if I keep this, do you?" Zola said, holding up the bottle of liquor.

Dean shook his head and let it fall back against the car seat. He looked like he was going into some sort of trance.

Sally and Zola walked slowly toward the school lawn. They took off their high heels and sat cross-legged on a concrete bench.

"So were you getting down with James Dean?" Zola asked.

"No. He had some things on his mind," Sally said.

"Oh," Zola said. She took a long sip of the Jägermeister, then offered it to Sally, but Sally shook her head. Zola drank some more. She wanted to drink until her mind went numb and she could no longer recapture the image of what she'd seen in the limo. "God, this tastes bad," she said, taking another giant gulp.

"Did you find Evan?" Sally asked.

Zola took the bottle away from her lips so she could answer. "Yes, Sally, I did find Evan. I found him all right. I found him in quite a compromising position." She took another swig. "In the back of a limousine with Skank McPherson sitting on his lap."

"Claudia Choney?" Sally said.

Zola nodded. "The one and only."

Zola realized what she'd said rhymed and suddenly the whole thing seemed hilariously funny and she started to laugh. Then Sally started laughing, too. Tears were running down their faces, and Zola's stomach hurt. Zola didn't know why she was laughing. This was turning out to be the worst night of her life and all she could do was sit there laughing hysterically.

"Oh, Sally," Zola said, when she was finally able to catch her breath. "I'm sorry you didn't get your big kiss."

"Yeah," Sally said. She wiped her eyes and scratched at her crotch where the Nair had burned her skin.

"Well, I love you, anyway," Zola said. She leaned in and gave Sally a very long, slow, drunken, closed-eyed, openmouthed kiss. Sally sat frozen, with her blue eyes opened wide. What the hell was this?

Zola sat back and took another swig from the bottle. "There," she said, "now you've been kissed at the prom. Congratufuckinglations. Come on, let's go back inside."

Carrying the bottle, she stood up and began staggering back to the school.

12

(**Coochie-man Sandwich**)

Olivia opened the side door to the gym and looked around for her friends. The "Our Hearts Will Go On" techno dance remix boomed from the speakers while The Stormy Knights took a break. Olivia couldn't believe it. She and Bill had had sex twice and they'd been playing the same song the first time. She felt like she was losing her mind.

Bill was still upstairs in the bio lab, tap-tap-tapping on a keyboard. The second time they'd done it, Bill had been on top, staring at the plastic model of the human brain, which was in pieces on the table behind Olivia's head. The medulla was lying on its side, and right when he climaxed Bill had a eureka lightbulb moment. "Medulla oblongata!" he shouted, climbing off Olivia and rushing over to the nearest computer. He told her he'd thought of something for his AP bio paper and he just had to get it down before he lost his train of thought. Olivia knew the medulla oblongata was the direct link to the spinal cord and all the nerve endings in the human body. Bill's paper was titled "The Science of Pleasure." Maybe he'd come up with a hypothesis for why he could orgasm twice in twenty minutes. His medulla oblongata was tremendous.

Olivia left Bill alone in the lab, hoping to find Min, Zola, and Sally so they could go crazy and dance together, even if the music was lame. But when she got to the gym, she changed her mind.

Min was chasing after Ozzy with a big wad of toilet paper in her hand. Every time she got close to wiping his little bottom, the Yorkie would scurry away to make a new mess on the floor. Zola and Sally were standing by the wall and they looked miserable. Sally was pale and glassy-eyed and Zola swayed unsteadily, obviously drunk, her face contorted in a sneer. Olivia adjusted her underwear and began to push her way through the crowd. For once, she would be the one coming to the rescue.

"Stupid mutt!" Jen Weaver screamed as Ozzy peed on her dyed-to-match pale pink satin shoe. "Your disgusting dog peed on my shoe!" she shouted at Tobias.

Jesus, Min thought, glaring at Jen. Someone should just shoot her and put her out of her misery. She'll never make it in the real world.

"He only peed a little," Tobias said. He held out his arms to his little sick dog. "Come here, boy; come to

Daddy." He puckered up his lips, and all of a sudden it occurred to Min that those were the very same lips she'd been kissing.

A couple of kids sniggered and Min's face grew hot with embarrassment.

"Tobias," Min hissed, and grabbed his arm. "You're ruining my prom."

"Excuse me? Aren't you being a little bit selfish?" Tobias said. "Can't you put anyone else's needs before your own for even one minute? That's what I get for going out with a high school girl."

Min felt her lower lip protruding in a girlish pout and she sucked it back in. Maybe Tobias was right. Maybe she was being immature. But Tobias didn't have to be so mean about it. Tears welled up in her eyes and her lower lip stuck out once more.

Suddenly Olivia, Sally, and Zola were at Min's side. They were like Charlie's Angels, Min thought. She couldn't have been happier to see them.

"Come on, Min," Olivia said.

"Fine, go with your friends," Tobias scoffed. "The witches of fucking Eastwick."

Olivia wanted to slap him. "Tobias, why don't you take Ozzy home to watch The Home Shopping Network and leave Min alone so she can enjoy herself for once?" she said instead.

Jen Weaver and the other five girls who constituted the prom planning committee approached them. They were all wearing blue plastic sapphire *Titanic* necklaces and they looked like freaks.

"Would you mind taking your little wrestling match outside?" Jen said. "I believe there's a bus in the parking lot waiting to take you all straight to the *Jerry Springer Show*."

"Why don't you go fuck yourself, Jen? Because you know no one else will," Olivia spat. She'd been waiting for years to say that line. She'd heard Zola say it to Alicia Burns on the bus trip to Washington, D.C., in eighth grade and thought it was the coolest mean thing she'd ever heard anyone say.

Just then Zola looked up and saw Evan and Claudia Choney. They were standing in a cardboard lifeboat in the corner, kissing and slow dancing, clearly unaware that the music had stopped. Zola's stomach clenched. She tried to look away but she couldn't. She couldn't believe they had the nerve to do that right in front of the whole school. It was humiliating. Evan's hand was on Claudia's thigh, inside the high slit of her long skirt. She licked his neck with her hideous pierced tongue. Zola looked around for Scott, Claudia's date, to see what he thought about the whole thing. He was sitting on the gym floor in the corner with three other guys from the football team, obliterated on punch.

It wasn't worth having a boyfriend if you felt this bad when it was over. As good as it had felt when it was happening—watching *The Matrix* twice in a row and imitating Keanu Reeves, picking blueberries naked on the banks of Nine Springs, sleeping over on Saturday nights when his parents were out of town and eating Pop-Tarts on Sunday, wearing his T-shirts—was as bad as she felt now. Zola hadn't been that nice to Evan lately, but she had planned to make it up to him. Now that skank had ruined everything, Zola thought drunkenly. Claudia had ruined her life.

The band started up again, playing "Our Hearts Will Go On" jungle style this time. Zola felt like she was going to puke. Out of nowhere Dean and his friend Jake swooped onto the dance floor, grabbed Sally, and trapped her in a coochie-man sandwich, pulsating their pelvises on either side of her. Zola stared at them, completely enthralled, while some of her classmates formed a circle around them and started clapping and whooping. Sally tried to get away, but Dean swiveled down to his knees in front of her and Jake gyrated against her ass, flailing his arms like he was riding a rodeo bull.

Then Zola noticed that Sally's nose was bleeding. Poor, delicate Sally was overwhelmed.

"Bathroom call!" Zola trumpeted, and dove into the fray to rescue her friend.

(13)

(Born Yesterday)

Zola grabbed a peach pashmina shawl from a nearby fashion victim, pressed it up against Sally's nose, and led her to the girls' room with Min and Olivia right behind them.

"Well, isn't this night just fabulous?" Zola said.

"At least it's all up from here," Min said.

"Is it?" Zola asked. She tried to imagine what tomorrow would be like. She'd wake up alone in her bed and turn on her morning song—"Strutter," by Kiss. Then she wouldn't call Evan like she usually did. Evan would probably be waking up to Claudia's nasty skank face. Zola would never call Evan again.

"You're not implying that we're peaking, are you?" Min said.

"All I'm saying is we don't know what's going to happen to us. I mean none of us would ever have guessed that our prom night would turn out to be this much of a nightmare," Zola said.

"At least your nose isn't bleeding and you don't have Dante's inferno between your legs thanks to you Nair fiends." Sally sniffed through the pashmina shawl. "It really burns."

"We know you wouldn't let anything else of Dante's between your legs," Min said.

Zola felt terrible for bullying Sally into using the Nair. "Hey, I've got some baby powder," she slurred. "Do you want some?" She always carried baby powder in the summer to put under her arms when she got sweaty. She loved the way it smelled. She'd bought a huge container of it at Costco, but it was too big to lug around, so she'd put some in a Ziploc to carry in her purse.

Zola touched Sally's arm and Sally recoiled at her touch. She still couldn't believe Zola had kissed her. And Zola was acting like nothing had happened. Sally wished that were true.

"Why do these things always happen to me?" Sally exclaimed, flapping her dress to fan her crotch.

Min grabbed the bag of powder out of Zola's hand and tossed it to Sally. "Don't be such a victim. You don't want them making a Lifetime Television for Women movie about you, do you?" Min said.

"Besides, you still have us," Olivia chimed in.

All four girls crowded into a stall with Zola's plastic baggie of baby powder. Sally dipped her fingers in the powder and hiked up her skirt to apply it to her sensitive bikini line. She tried to keep her head back so the blood would stop running from her nose, but she could feel another drip coming.

Someone entered the girls' room and lit a cigarette.

"Keep your head back, Sally," Zola instructed. "The bleeding hasn't stopped yet."

"Is everything all right?" the woman smoking the cigarette asked. It was Miss McCormack, the music teacher. She was always trying to be a "friend" to the girls. Once she had offered to teach Sally how to drive in her new Volkswagen Beetle and once she had suggested a sleep over at her house. The girls thought she was insane.

Sally swiped at her nose. The last thing she needed was to get blood on her dress. Her talcy fingers left a clumpy button of the white powder right on the tip of her nose just as Miss McCormack peered over the top of the stall door.

"Hey, I'm not going to say anything, you guys, but it would be cool if you took your coke outside," Miss McCormack said. "I don't want to get you suspended right before graduation, if you know what I'm saying. We'll just make this our little secret."

"It's not what you think, Miss McCormack," Zola said.

"Hey, girls, I wasn't born yesterday, but I also wasn't born so long ago that I don't know what's going on in this school."

"Whatever you say," Zola answered, trying to keep a straight face. Miss McCormack is such a bonehead lame-ass loser, she thought drunkenly.

The girls unlocked the door and piled out.

"Actually, you'd better give me that," Miss McCormack said, holding out her hand.

"But Miss McCormack . . . ," Zola said.

"I'm afraid I have to put my foot down about this." Zola looked down at Miss McCormack's feet. What were those, Easy Spirit shoes?

Zola shrugged and handed her the bag of baby powder. They left the bathroom but turned just in time to see Miss McCormack making a line of the talc on the edge of the sink.

"I see what you mean about life going downhill," Min said to Zola as they headed back into the gym.

They got there just in time to see Jen Weaver, wearing a hokey life jacket, start walking toward the stage to announce the prom king and queen. Ozzy ran under her feet and she tripped and fell back into the arms of Dan Giddings, who was attempting to light a cigarette. He threw his match into his date's dried flower corsage, which burst into flames, causing her to pull it off and throw it on the floor. Then the paper tablecloth on the buffet table caught fire, and the sprinkler system went off.

Water started pouring down from the tiny spigots in

the pipes running along the gym ceiling. Everyone was screaming and getting soaked. Jen and the rest of the prom planning committee looked distraught, but they should have been happy, Min thought. The prom's theme was a success. It really did look like the *Titanic*.

Only old man Otis had reason to be upset. "My floor!" he moaned. "My beautiful new gym floor!" Min felt sorry for him. All this water was going to make it warp.

Poor Ozzy didn't like to get wet. He ran sheepishly over to Tobias and Tobias swept him up in a tearful burst of emotion. Min watched as the happy couple was reunited. Ozzy's tail wagged furiously as he licked every inch of Tobias's face. They looked like a young couple in love, kissing in the rain. They were more romantic than Leonardo DiCaprio and Kate Winslet—they wouldn't mind drowning as long as they could be together.

"Let's get out of here," Zola said. But she was so drunk, she fell. Her mother's pearls got caught on her purse as she broke her fall and tore from her neck. Pearls rolled everywhere.

Zola's mother used to wear those pearls every day and she had given them to Zola the day she died. Zola only wore them on special occasions because she was too afraid of breaking them but everyone knew they were her most prized possession. They were all she had left of her mother.

The girls scrambled to pick them all up, crawling on their hands and knees in their prom dresses. Even Olivia got down on her knees to help, despite the fact that the water would ruin her hair for good. It was curling by the second but she didn't care anymore—she had to help Zola find the pearls. The girls were getting soaked, but they kept searching until they were sure they had collected every last one.

(14)

(Swimsuits Optional)

None of the girls had ever seen Zola cry. Not even when her mother died, although they were sure she had, just not in front of them. She stood in front of Min's car, looking into her beaded purse at her mother's loose pearls. What if she hadn't found all of them? What if one of the pearls, the only remnants she had of her mother, was left in the La Follette High gym? What if some loser picked it up and stuck it in his pocket, or Otis wrung it out of his filthy mop into a bucket and down a drain, or it got lodged in the sole of someone's Nike?

"You can have them restrung," Min said.

"I know," Zola said. She wiped her eyes. "I don't know what's wrong with me. I'm not myself." But the pearls wouldn't be the same once they were restrung, she thought. It wouldn't be the same string that had been around her mother's neck.

Zola was right, Sally thought, she wasn't herself.

"Well, that was beyond lame," Olivia said. "And my hair is totally ruined." It looked like there had been an explosion on her head.

"I feel a little bad leaving without saying good-bye to Tobias," Min said. "Maybe I should go back and tell him we're going."

"Forget it," Zola said. She couldn't believe Min was actually thinking of going back into that hellhole. "He's happy in there dancing with Ozzy. Maybe *they'll* be the prom king and queen."

"Ozzy's a boy," Min reminded her.

"What are we going to do now?" Sally asked.

"Maybe we should go back to Min's house and dye her hair the same color as Ozzy's so her boyfriend will finally pay attention to her," Zola said.

"What do you think they call that color?" Olivia asked.

"Yorkie rust red," Zola said.

"Terrier tawny," Min replied, laughing. "And you've made your point, by the way."

"Hey, look at the stars," Sally interrupted them, pointing up at the sky.

The girls looked up at the black sky. The stars were so magnificent, they were silent for a moment.

"What's that?" Olivia said.

"What?" Zola said.

Olivia pointed at a white streak dividing the sky. It

seemed to come straight down to Earth from the center of the moon. "That," she said. "That long strip of fog."

"It looks almost like tire tracks from a bike," Min said.

"That's weird."

"It really does."

"I'm hungry," Min said. "Of course the whole world could be coming to an end and I'd still be hungry."

"Well, a girl's gotta eat," Zola said. She wouldn't have minded drowning her sorrows in a gigantic strawberry milk shake from Stewart's. "I feel a Stewart's run coming on," she growled, beating her chest like Tarzan.

"I might as well put back the ten pounds I lost for this stupid prom," Min said, unlocking the car.

"You have freshman year at college to do that," Olivia commented.

They got into the Mitzvah Mobile, Min in the driver's seat with Zola next to her and Sally and Olivia in the back.

"Can we please *not* go to Stewart's?" Olivia said from the backseat. *"Please?"* She could just imagine what losers they'd look like, all dressed up with nothing to do but stuff their faces in the parking lot at Stewart's.

"And what would you suggest we do, Miss Smarty Drop-your-pants McGraw?" Min asked.

"What about Jason Altman's after party?" Olivia suggested, leaning into the front seat. She hadn't planned on swimming before because she didn't want her hair to get wet, but now it was wet anyway. She might as well enjoy herself.

"But it's not after yet. It's more like during," Min said, still heading down Johnson Street toward Stewart's.

Sally leaned forward and rested her chin on the back of Zola's seat. She was tired of all her friends' bickering. "Let's just go to the goddamned party," she said in a voice that didn't even sound like her own.

"Woo-hoo! Right on, Sally!" Zola screeched out her open window.

"You party animal!" Min howled.

She turned on the radio and "Our Hearts Will Go On" blasted into the car. They all screamed and Zola scrambled to change the station.

Min turned down a long dirt road, following the directions on the printed out e-vitation Jason had e-mailed everyone. What a freak. He had written *swimsuits optional* and Min could just imagine him jerking off while he hit send.

"So, Sally, you wild woman," Min said. "Did you hook up with Dean? Is that why you're so footloose and fancy free this evening?"

Sally was actually having second thoughts about how she'd treated Dean. Maybe she'd been too hard on him. Girls were always saying that boys should be sensitive and show their feelings and allow themselves to cry. Maybe it was a good thing that he felt comfortable enough with her to cry in front of her like that. Maybe it was a compliment. She had been so mean to him, calling him annoying. It just didn't seem particularly masculine to be bawling his eyes out about leaving high school. He probably hated her now and that's why he'd acted like such a jerk with his stupid friend on the dance floor. If he came to the after party she would try to talk to him and tell him she was sorry for being so insensitive.

"Well?" Min said. "Did you get your first kiss?"

Sally didn't know what to say. Figures that her big kiss would be from Zola. "It wasn't my first kiss," she said.

"So you did get kissed!" Olivia crowed.

Sally didn't say anything. For the rest of the trip she played the incident with Zola over and over in her mind. What had it meant? Did Zola like her in that way? Had she wanted to kiss her for a long time or was she just drunk? She didn't want her only kiss in high school to be from a girl. She wished she could have a moment alone with Zola so she could ask her about it. But she was scared to even look at Zola, let alone talk to her. Did this mean she was a lesbian? Or did it mean she wasn't? She looked at her reflection in the car window. What she really wanted to do right now was write in her diary.

Zola, if you ever read this, I'm sorry, but I really wish you hadn't kissed me. How is any boy ever going to fall in love with me if I'm a lesbian?

15

(Karma)

There was no one there when they got to Jason Altman's house, not even Jason's parents. They were away for the entire weekend.

The girls changed into their swimsuits in the empty cabana and grabbed their towels. They'd made a point of bringing their own towels. Anything belonging to Jason Altman could very well be seriously diseased.

Min took her cell phone out of her purse. "I'm going to call Tobias and see if he got home all right," she said.

"Spare us," Zola said, and started walking toward the strip of pebbly beach behind the house.

Tobias wasn't home. The phone rang and rang and finally the machine picked up. Min left a message in their usual puppy talk. "I wuff you," she said, and hung up.

It felt strange to be wearing a bathing suit and lying on the beach at night.

Olivia began to wonder if it was a good idea to get

there so early. Maybe they'd look like dorks when the other kids showed up, being the first ones there. Maybe no one was even going to come. Maybe something really cool got put together somewhere else at the last minute, and there the four of them were, by themselves, like the biggest geeks in the universe.

Sally regretted leaving her diary in the car. There was enough moonlight to see, and she had so much to write.

Min missed Tobias and Ozzy. Ozzy loved the beach as long as he didn't have to get wet. She couldn't wait to see Tobias so they could have make-up sex. She lay clutching her cell phone, checking to make sure it was still juiced up.

And Zola was too drunk to really care where she was. She wished she could do the whole prom over. She wished she had been the one kissing Evan instead of that skank. She wondered if Evan was thinking about her at all.

Sometimes being with your girlfriends was the best feeling in the world. There wasn't anyplace in the universe you would rather be than laughing and bitching and gossiping with your girls. But sometimes you just needed to see your boyfriend.

"Do you think there's one single cool guy in Madison?" Zola asked sleepily.

"Lenny," Sally said.

"Who is Lenny?" Olivia said.

"The guy on the motorcycle outside the school. Lenny Kravitz," Sally said.

"Sally, I'm surprised you didn't run up and jump on the back of his bike," Min said. "You could have gotten his autograph."

Sally laughed in an overtired punchy way. "Lenny. Lenny," she repeated.

"Clarence Terence," a voice said, coming toward them. "And I don't do autographs. Too cheesy."

Sally sat up and stared, her mouth falling open. She nudged Min sharply with her elbow. It was *him*.

"Where is everybody?" he asked. "I thought this was supposed to be a party."

"We're early," Zola said, rolling over. "And you know what they say," she added, squinting at him seductively. "The early bird catches the worm."

"I'll be delivering the pearls of wisdom, if you don't mind," Clarence said. "Speaking of which, I have something that belongs to you." He handed Zola one of her mother's pearls.

"Thank you," she said, astonished.

"But you shouldn't be so afraid of losing things. You should bury that pearl in the sand or toss it into the lake. All things have a way of coming back to us," he said. "It's called karma."

Zola was grateful to get the pearl back but she didn't appreciate the little New Age speech. He didn't know that the pearls had belonged to her mother. Who the hell was this guy, anyway?

"What are you, some kind of foreign exchange student?" Zola asked. "Were you left back a few years or something?"

"You could say that," Clarence Terence said, trying to maintain his patience. "Left back a few thousand or skipped forward a few thousand. It depends on how you look at it."

Now that he was here he wished he'd made a more dramatic entrance so the girls would treat him with a bit more respect. He could have zoomed in from the Milky Way like E.T. or walked up out of the lake like the Creature from the Black Lagoon. That would have gotten their attention.

"Who are you?" Olivia asked. "If you're going to crash this party you should at least introduce yourself."

"Yeah, you look like Lenny Kravitz, but you sound more like Yanni," Min said.

Now that hurt. Clarence was sure he had thought of everything but he hadn't counted on these girls being so difficult. He had thought they would be thrilled to see him. He had felt like he was a one-man Make-A-Wish Foundation. He had felt like Madonna must feel calling

random people in the Los Angeles phone book and saying, "Hi, this is Madonna; that's right, Madonna, and I'm
calling to make your day." He had felt like Ed McMahon,
only young and good-looking, with a giant Publishers
Clearing House check and a small bunch of balloons.

He didn't expect to be treated like some sort of door-to-
door Jehovah's Witness. Or the new neighborhood Megan's
law pervert. Or some kind of substitute teacher freak.

He had frankly forgotten how bitchy four seventeen-
year-old girls could get when they were together. It had been
a long time since he had experienced it firsthand. From now
on maybe he would deal with them one at a time.

"I'm your fairy godmother," Clarence said.

The girls' eyebrows all shot up and they glanced at
each other, giggling.

"You're gay?" Zola asked.

"No, I'm not gay," Clarence said, putting his hands on
his hips.

"You call yourself a fairy godmother, you're wearing a
white leather jacket," Min said, "and you want us to think
you're not gay?"

"It doesn't matter what you think of me. It only matters
what you think of yourself."

"Well, Miss Fairy Godmother or whatever you are, it's
almost midnight and you're still here and we're already
sort of over it," Zola said, standing up on her towel. "I

don't know about you girls, but I'm going for a midnight swim before I turn into a pumpkin. Bye." She ran toward the water. The other girls ran after her.

Only Sally turned around. "Bye, Lenny," she said, waving.

"Don't call me Lenny," he yelled after her. How could the girls just leave him standing there? He hadn't even come close to doing what he came for, and now he was extremely irritated.

Breathe, he told himself. He remembered something he'd read in that book, *The Buddha at Work:* "Think of discouragement as opportunity." He would have to try again later. And he'd be sure to make a better entrance next time.

(16)

(Itsy-Bitsy Teeny-Weeny)

The girls treaded water in the icy lake. Zola's and Sally's legs accidentally touched for a moment and Sally looked at Zola meaningfully but Zola didn't say anything. She seemed oblivious. Sally felt very aware of her own body. Her breasts were sort of floaty in the water and she hoped they would stay in her suit. The last thing she wanted was to have Zola staring at her bare breasts. She blushed in the dark for having such perverted lesbian thoughts. God, she had a lot to work out in her diary.

Min had decided to swim holding her cell phone up overhead so she wouldn't miss Tobias's call. She looked like a chubby version of the only brown-haired female on *Baywatch,* rescuing something from the dangerous waters of LA.

Zola sank in a dead man's float. Before their mother died, she used to scare her little brother, Nathaniel, on purpose with the dead man's float. He would scream and yell, "Zola, stop drownding! Stop drownding!" She didn't do that with Nathaniel anymore, but with her friends it was okay. It felt good to be completely submerged.

Olivia watched Zola sink in the moonlit water and dunked her head under in an act of total abandon. The cold water felt wonderful on her scalp.

Min's cell phone rang. It was strange to hear the ring against the sound of the croaking frogs and the chirping crickets and the gentle splashing of water. Zola and Olivia popped their heads out of the lake like seals.

"You really shouldn't answer that, Min," Zola said.

The phone rang again.

"I know, but I miss him," Min said.

"He's a loser," Zola said. "Look at the way he treated you at your own *prom*."

"Since when are you so *prom*itically correct?" Min said.

"You should throw the phone in the water," Zola said.

"You sound like Lenny Kravitz over there," Olivia said. "But it's not a bad idea, Min. It's the only way you won't be tempted to answer."

"Give me the phone," Zola said. She grabbed it out of Min's hand.

Min tried to grab it back and Zola handed it to Olivia. The phone stopped ringing. "Give it back," Min demanded.

"No," Olivia said. "Don't call him back. He needs to be punished. You have to rub his nose in it."

"Whose nose? Tobias's or Ozzy's?" Zola said.

"Please hand me the phone," Min whined.

"I'll give it to Sally. She won't do anything with it and she'll give it back to you later." Olivia gave the phone to Sally.

"How do you know I won't do anything with it?" Sally asked, annoyed. "Maybe I'll drop it in the lake."

"You wouldn't do that, Sally," Min said. "Anyway, you like Tobias, don't you?"

"No, Min, I don't like Tobias," Sally said.

Zola and Olivia laughed. The phone rang again.

"And frankly this fucking phone is ruining my relaxing swim," Sally said, her teeth chattering. She held the ringing phone high over her head and then tossed it far into the lake. It splashed and sank.

All three girls looked at Sally with their mouths open in shock.

Sally couldn't believe she'd done it, either. "Don't forget what Lenny said," she said, giggling. "Everything has a way of coming back to you." She turned and floated on her back, trying to keep herself from bursting into a giggling fit. Once she started, she couldn't stop.

Zola started to howl with laughter and Sally turned over, accidentally swallowing water. She choked and coughed, a trail of yellow snot dangling from her nose. When Olivia saw it she started laughing uncontrollably. Then Min noticed it, too, and she screeched with laughter. Sally could no longer hold back her giggling fit and she splashed to stay afloat. The girls were like hysterical hyenas. They couldn't stop. They laughed so hard they got stomachaches and could barely swim.

"Oh God!" Min shouted. "Make it stop!"

But that only got them laughing harder.

It was one of those moments they would remember for the rest of their lives.

By the time they got out of the water, Clarence Terence was gone.

They were standing and shivering, wrapped in their towels, when Jason Altman showed up. He was wearing an itsy-bitsy teeny-weeny yellow bikini, sans polka dots. It looked really obscene.

"So you girls are the only ones who showed," Jason said, his green eyes bugging out of his head. He clapped. "Cool!"

The girls looked at each other. Jesus.

"Want to go back in the water, Zola?" Jason asked in what he probably thought was his sexiest voice.

"Actually, we were just leaving," Zola said, turning away.

"Sure you're not tempted?" Jason asked. "I don't think Evan will mind. He's got his hands fulla Choney. Get it?"

"Shut up," Zola snapped. "Come on," she said to the other girls, and started walking toward the car.

"What about you, Sally?" Jason asked, staring at Sally's chest. "Feel like a swim?"

"Uh—uh . . . ," Sally stammered.

"That would be a no," Min said.

"Oh, I'm sorry, I didn't know Sal here was incapable of speaking," Jason said.

Sally was sick of her friends always speaking for her. They gave her a hard time about being a virgin but then they never gave her a chance to be alone with a boy for even five minutes. If it hadn't been for Zola coming over to Dean's car and grabbing his Jägermeister, things might have worked out very differently with Dean.

"I can speak for myself," she said, glaring at the other girls.

"Okay, Sally," Min said. "I'm sorry. Why don't you stay and hang out here for a while with Jason and we'll see you tomorrow?"

Sally played the scene out in her mind. She could stay alone with Jason. Go for a swim. They could kiss. Maybe even have sex.

Jason stood there gawking at her with his spiky red hair and chin scar. Suddenly she felt dizzy.

"Bye, you two," Olivia said as she and Min followed Zola to Min's car.

"Bye!" Jason called.

Sally started to see black and her knees began to buckle. "Wait!" she screamed. Coming to her senses, she broke into a run and beat the other girls to the car.

⊙17

(The Four Pigs)

The girls got to Min's house a little after midnight but Min's parents were still surprised to see them home so soon. Since it was prom night, Rabbi Weinstock had given Min permission to stay out as late as she wanted and he had joked that it would be nice to see her by next Tuesday.

"Well?" he said. "How was it?" They looked at him blankly. "That bad, huh?" he said. "Are you hungry?"

"We're starving," Min said.

"I know *you're* starving," her father said. "You're always starving. Would your friends like something to eat?" Min hit him playfully on the arm.

"We're all starving, Steve," Zola said. "It's been a hellish night."

"Hellish!" Rabbi Weinstock said. "Well, what can I do to make things better?"

"Will you make us pancakes like you used to when we

were kids? In the shape of our initials?" Zola asked. She asked so sweetly, Min's father suddenly remembered all those sleepovers the girls used to have. Watching *The Wizard of Oz* and eating bowls of popcorn, singing while he played piano, and all those noisy pancake breakfasts. He almost felt like crying.

"Pancakes it is," he trumpeted, tying on his silly Chef Dad apron and brandishing the spatula.

"And there are towels in the bathroom cupboard if you want to take showers," Mrs. Weinstock offered. She was wearing her beautiful green silk robe. The one the girls had all tried on. It had fit Olivia best because she was the smallest, and Mrs. Weinstock was small, too. For the millionth time, Olivia admired Min's mother's graceful poise. It was Olivia's goal in life to appear as serene and feminine as Mrs. Weinstock. She had a long way to go.

The girls took showers and changed into their pre-prom clothes. Then they went downstairs to the kitchen. Rabbi Weinstock slid a blueberry pancake in the shape of a giant *Z* onto Zola's plate. Mrs. Weinstock poured hot syrup from a sauce pot into a pretty green pitcher. By the time the other girls finished their *M, O,* and *S,* Zola was ready for another *Z* and the rabbi gladly indulged her.

"You girls have been friends for a long time," Mrs. Weinstock said.

"Duh," Min said with her mouth full.

"I think we should have a toast to your friendship," her mother said. She took a bottle of Taittinger's out of the fridge and poured everyone a glass in tall champagne flutes.

Olivia was amazed. Her mother would have offered them soy milk. *Chocolate* soy milk, maybe, if it was a special occasion. She loved the taste of the Taittinger's. She had a poster of Marilyn Monroe with a bottle of Taittinger's champagne in her room.

"To friendship," Min's mother said, raising her glass. "To the four of you girls."

The girls raised their glasses. "To us," they chorused.

Sleepy and tipsy, Min, Olivia, Zola, and Sally headed downstairs to crash in the Weinstocks' rumpus room. Min plugged in the air mattress and pressed a button. "As seen on TV," she said as it inflated in less than a minute. "This is me before my period," Min joked. "A little bloated."

The mattress was queen-size and there was a pull-out couch, too. When they were little they had all slept on the pullout together, but now they were too big to fit comfortably.

"I'll sleep on the air mattress," Min said.

"I'll try it with you," Olivia said. "The sofa bed isn't good for my back."

"Fooling around with Bill in the bio lab closet isn't good for your back, either, but you do that," Min joked.

"At least I don't have to kiss two dogs. Do you ever roll over and kiss Ozzy by mistake, thinking he's Tobias?" Olivia answered. She glanced at Zola to back her up.

"Ozzy's probably a better kisser," Zola said, not disappointing her.

"Well, he does use a lot more tongue." Min laughed.

Sally didn't know what to do. If Olivia and Min took the air mattress, that left the sofa bed to her and Zola. She must have slept in the same bed with Zola dozens of times but now things were different. Since the kiss. She couldn't spend the night in a bed with Zola. What if Zola tried to kiss her again? What if she tried to do more?

Zola was already putting a sheet on the bed, laughing each time the same elasticized corner popped off the mattress.

"I think I'll sleep on the floor," Sally said.

"Why?" Min said. "You and Zola can have the pullout. It's huge."

"I prefer the floor," Sally insisted.

"But the sleeping bag's in the attic and we don't have enough blankets," Min said. "Come on, Sally. The pullout's comfortable."

"What, do I smell or something?" Zola said, sniffing under her arms. "You're the one who snores."

Sally tried to give Zola a meaningful look, a how-can-you-pretend-that-nothing-happened look, but Zola just looked back at her and said, "What?"

Zola didn't know what had come over Sally. She had no idea why she was acting so strange. Being a virgin for so long was obviously beginning to fry her brain.

Min went upstairs and came back down with another bottle of Taittinger's and an old photo album. She had checked her answering machine, but there was no message from Tobias. She decided to try not to think about him until tomorrow.

The girls sat cross-legged on the floor and passed around the photo album. In it they were children: swinging on the tire in the Weinstocks' backyard; eating lobster at a fish restaurant; at the Kitefest; at the Madison Zoo; at their birthday parties; at Min's bas mitzvah.

They'd had so much fun that day. Zola's mom hadn't gotten sick yet and Olivia's parents were still together. Sally was proudly wearing the nerdiest purple-flowered Laura Ashley dress, which she would probably still be wearing if the other girls hadn't refused to hang out with her if she did. "We don't want to be enablers," Zola had said.

At her bas mitzvah, Min had gotten tons of cash from her relatives, and her father was so proud, he couldn't stop crying the whole day. And Zola had sat on a boy's lap for the first time. It was Min's older cousin, Howard. He had offered Zola a drink and she made out with him in a phone booth in the hotel where the reception took place. They kissed under the bright light on the phone booth ceiling that went on when they shut the door and he put his hand up her dress.

"Remember the pact?" Min asked.

On the night of Min's bas mitzvah they had sat on the floor in the rumpus room and made a pact that they would always be friends. They called themselves the Four Pigs then and they each wore an item of pink clothing every day. Zola had gotten a can of diet Coke from the Weinstocks' pantry and they passed it around the circle, each vowing solemnly that the Four Pigs would stay together forever. Then they put the can of diet Coke in a Nike shoe box and swore they would drink it together in ten years.

"We were such dorks," Olivia said.

"Losers," Zola added.

"Do you still have the shoe box, Min?" Sally asked.

"I think it's upstairs in the attic," Min said.

That was where the sleeping bag was. "Why don't we go get it?" Sally said. "Maybe there'll be some other cool stuff and we can grab the sleeping bag, too."

"What's with you and the sleeping bag?" Min said.

"Nothing," Sally said defensively.

"Well, even if high school was suck city at least we are still friends," Min said, trying to cheer everyone up.

"And we did have a lot of fun," Olivia said. She looked around at her friends' glum faces and decided she sounded a little too perky. "Kind of," she added.

"It's only high school, anyway," Zola said. "We've got the rest of our lives ahead of us."

"Right," Olivia said, taking a drink of champagne. She handed her glass to Sally, who gulped down what was left.

"Right." Sally burped, and the other girls giggled.

They finished the bottle of champagne and reminisced a while longer. Before they knew it the sun was almost coming up. Finally they got under the covers.

Except for Sally. There was no way she was going to sleep without writing at least one paragraph in her diary. She grabbed her backpack and slipped into the bathroom. She wrote as fast as she could, about everything that had happened that night.

When she was done, she came out of the bathroom and walked around to her side of the bed. She lay down gingerly on top of the covers.

"Don't you want to be under the blanket?" Zola asked.

Sally got under the blanket and lay as far out on the edge of the mattress as she could get without falling out. She didn't feel any better after writing in her diary. It only made her want to talk.

"What's up, Sally?" Zola whispered.

Sally didn't answer.

"Want me to tell you about the time I shoplifted from Victoria's Secret?" Zola offered.

"No." Min groaned. They had all heard the story a thousand times.

"Come on," Zola begged.

Somewhere near the point in the story where Zola put the purple garter belt on, pulled her jeans on over it, and smiled at the horny old security guard, Min, Olivia, Sally, and Zola herself all fell fast asleep. Even the purr of a motorcycle, somewhere very close by, didn't wake them.

(Rated R for Wretched)

Clarence Terence entered the Weinstocks' rec room and looked around. He decided to shoot a little pool while he thought about his game plan. He grabbed a stick from the wall, lifted the wooden triangle from around the balls, and broke. The pool table was Rabbi Weinstock's pride and joy. He liked to play pool with the cantor for money. He had wanted the room to look woody and masculine but his wife had made giant flowery pillows and strewn them everywhere and used a sponge technique to paint the walls. The antique sewing machine resting on the white wicker table in the corner also ruined the effect.

The girls were sound asleep and Clarence wanted them to stay that way. They were definitely more lovable when they were sleeping. Min was snoring softly and Olivia was just a big mop of frizzy hair. Sally was lying stiff as a board on the edge of the bed and Zola was sleeping so peacefully she looked like she was about six. Her face had lost its toughness.

He glanced at Min's photo album and then turned on the TV to *Behind the Music*—"Madonna." He strummed his guitar quietly, playing along to "Rescue Me."

"And you want us to think you're not gay," Zola said, sitting up in bed.

Let the games begin. "Hi, Zola," Clarence Terence said, lifting his mirrored shades onto the top of his head. "Why are you giving me a hard time? Did Cinderella start berating her fairy godmother with insults? No, she was polite and grateful."

"What are you doing here?"

Clarence figured he might as well cut to the chase. "I'm here to present your future. It's a Clarence Terence Production, in vivid Technicolor, with surround sound, and it's rated R for wretched."

"Thanks a lot," Zola said sarcastically.

"It's *All About Eve* meets *Hardbodies* and we're appropriately heading toward Hollyweird, Los Angeles, LA, *Hell* A, La La Land."

LA. Now, that didn't sound so bad. Zola didn't know exactly what she wanted to do with her life, but she wanted it to be exciting. And LA sounded very exciting. She knew she was going to the University of Wisconsin, right here in Madison, with Min, Olivia, and Sally, and she hadn't thought much beyond that. She had wanted to stay in Madison so she wouldn't have to leave her little brother, Nathaniel. After college, she wanted a husband and children and a good career. To live in a place like LA, though, that would be cool.

"All right, Lenny, let's go," she said.

"My name isn't Lenny. It's Clarence." Clarence was disappointed. He had expected to be received with surprise and delight, but Zola was so matter-of-fact about talking to her fairy godmother, you'd think she did it every day. It kind of ruined the effect.

"Whatever," Zola said, yawning. "Can my friends come with us?"

"No, your future is yours and yours alone," he said. "Now lie down, clear your mind, and try to keep the wisecracking thoughts down to a minimum."

He strummed the chord for Zola on his guitar. He strummed it again. When he strummed it for the third time the two of them were driving in a white Cadillac convertible going south on Ventura Boulevard in Los Angeles, California.

(Cheer Up. It's Just the Future.)

Clarence's hands rested lightly on the wheel and the wind whipped through Zola's hair. The Los Angeles late afternoon sun felt lovely on her shoulders.

"Maybe we'll have time to go to the beach later," Clarence said.

"Cool," Zola said. "Now, what were you going to show me?"

"Just be patient," he said, looking at the car clock. "If everything goes according to schedule we should be coming up to you any second now."

"Coming up to me?" Zola asked.

Clarence glanced in the rearview mirror. "Here you are," he said.

Zola craned her neck to see but all she found was a public bus approaching. Clarence drove side by side with the bus. Zola looked up at the bus windows and saw a few men looking out, an old Chinese lady, and . . .

"That's me!" she said.

"That's right."

"Why would I be riding a bus?" Zola asked, mortified. Everyone in LA drove. Why didn't she have a great car? "Buses are for losers," she said.

"You can't drive," he said. "License revoked. DWI. Weekends spent picking up garbage on the side of the highway in a stylin' orange jumpsuit."

"I won't do that," Zola said. "I'd rather die."

"It's either that or cleaning bedpans at an old age home. No one said you didn't have a choice."

Zola looked up at her own face in the bus window. Her skin was tan and healthy looking. Her hair was long, with wispy bangs. Except for the hair, she looked pretty much the same.

"I look good," she said.

"Yes, you do. What did you expect? You'd turn into an old hag or something?"

"I was just sort of shaken up by the whole bus thing," she said.

"You look very good. In fact, you're a model."

"A model!" Zola said. People had always told her she was pretty enough to be a model but she had never really considered it. Her mother had always encouraged her not to focus on her looks. But being a model in LA certainly sounded glamorous. Things were definitely looking up.

Clarence drove past the bus and turned at the next light.

"Where are we going?" Zola asked.

Clarence rolled his eyes. "Just sit and watch. You must be really annoying to go to the movies with."

After several blocks, Clarence parked the car, in front of a mailbox with *The Fells* painted on its side. A fat Hispanic woman in a yellow maid's uniform was putting the recycling out front for the garbagemen to pick up. She went back in the house and Clarence and Zola slipped inside after her. A beautiful little girl, about five years old, ran toward them. She looked just like Evan. "Look what I made for Daddy," the little girl said to the maid, holding up a crayon drawing of a rainbow.

"That's nice," the maid said to the little girl. In the corner of the picture the little girl's teacher had written her name. Elizabeth Fell.

"That was my mother's name," Zola whispered to Clarence, her eyes welling up with tears.

"You don't have to whisper," he said. "They can't hear or see you."

"So Evan and I get married and move to Los Angeles and have a beautiful baby girl, who I name Elizabeth after my mother, and we live in this great house. And I'm a model! Cool!" Zola said.

"I'll keep the picture for you," the maid said, taking it

from the little girl. "Your daddy is recording at the studio. He'll be home late. But Mommy would like the picture, too, and she'll be home soon."

The studio! Evan had a record deal.

"I don't want Mommy to have my picture," the little girl insisted. "It's for Daddy."

How sweet! Zola thought. "I want to look around," she said to Clarence.

She went from room to room. First the living room. Sleek and modern with windows looking out at palm and banana trees. "Look," Zola said, picking up the La Follette High School yearbook. "It's funny. We haven't even gotten them yet. This is the first time I get to see it."

"We don't have a lot of time," Clarence said impatiently.

"Just let me look around a little longer."

She went upstairs to the little girl's room. There was a beautiful little bed with a duck-patterned quilt and a small table and chairs with a tea set ready to serve afternoon tea.

She wandered into the master bedroom. "Wow," Zola said to Clarence. "It looks like Barbie decorated this place." The room was huge, with pale pink carpeting and an enormous pink canopied bed. On the bedside table there was a strange photograph of a woman. Zola walked over to it and picked it up. Why would there be a picture of . . . Zola searched her mind for a name to match the face. The woman looked so familiar. Wait a minute. It was Claudia. *Claudia Choney*. Her hair was different, dyed red now, and she was sort of fat. Why would she and Evan have a picture of Claudia Choney on their bedside table?

Then Zola focused on another framed picture hanging on the wall over the bed. It was Evan and Claudia dressed in a tuxedo and wedding gown, kissing at the altar.

This was Claudia's bedroom, not her own. And that was Claudia's little girl, not hers. But what was she doing here? Why had Clarence taken her here?

She whirled around. "But where am I?" she asked him desperately. "Where was I going on that bus?"

Clarence pulled open a drawer in a huge white armoire. Inside were Evan's shirts, straight from the cleaners, folded around cardboard in symmetrical piles. Clarence lifted up a pile of shirts and pulled out a manila folder. Neatly tucked inside the folder was a magazine. A disgusting, second-rate men's magazine with a crotch shot centerfold. Clarence flipped through the pages until he found what he was looking for.

"Here you are," he said, handing the magazine to Zola.

It was a sleazy picture of herself with two other girls

wearing nothing but a shiny black leather thong. Her bare chest was just as tanned and oiled as the rest of her. "Oh my God," Zola said.

"Well, I said you were a model. I didn't exactly say you were a supermodel," Clarence said.

"Hi, sweetie!" It was Claudia. Her unmistakable skank voice ringing out throughout the house.

Zola ran downstairs and into the kitchen.

"Come to Mama, Elizabeth," Claudia called.

Elizabeth ran to her mother and gave her a hug.

Zola stood next to Clarence and watched in horror. Claudia was squeezed into brown suede pants, and there was a giant diamond rock on her fat finger. The phone rang and Claudia answered it. "Hi, honey," she said into the phone. "It's your father," she said to Elizabeth. "Evan, our plane leaves early tomorrow for Madison and I want us to be rested for the reunion." She licked her finger and rubbed at a spot on Elizabeth's cheek. Zola noticed Claudia wasn't wearing her tongue stud anymore. "Evan, just try to be here, all right?" she said, sounding exasperated, and hung up.

Zola shook her head at Clarence Terence. "I can't take any more of this," she said. "I have to get out of here." She ran out of the kitchen and sank onto Claudia's living-room couch, too stunned to speak.

"Cheer up. It's just the future," Clarence said, sitting

down next to her. "And the future is never more important than the present."

"Please," Zola begged, her head in her hands. "Tell me there's something good about all this. At least I'm still friends with Sally, Min, and Olivia, aren't I?"

Clarence picked a piece of lint out of one of his dreadlocks. "Just like in the movies, I can't answer all your questions, Zola," he said. "Let's just say our time is up and the credits are getting ready to roll."

"Take me home," Zola said. "Take me back to Min's house."

Clarence was disappointed. "Come on," he said. "I hate to come all the way to LA without going to the beach, or Disney, or catching a flick at Graumann's. My foot fits perfectly into Elvis's footprint, you know."

"Just get me out of here," Zola insisted, getting up and heading toward Claudia's front door.

The next thing she knew she was lying on the pullout sofa bed next to Sally, and Lenny, or whatever the hell his name was, was nowhere in sight. Zola was so glad to be back in the present, safe in bed in the Weinstocks' cozy rumpus room with her three best friends, that she squeezed herself up against Sally and gave her a gigantic hug.

Sally's eyes opened wide as she was jolted awake by the force of Zola's hug. There was a strange new odor in the room. Motor oil.

(Rated X for Exhausting)

As usual, Clarence was very behind. With only one future down, and three more to go, he still had a long night ahead of him.

Olivia had to be next because there were flight schedules involved.

Clarence lulled the extremely uptight Sally back to sleep with his guitar and then knelt on Olivia's side of the air mattress and softly serenaded her with Britney Spears's version of "I Can't Get No Satisfaction." Olivia didn't budge. She was out like a light. Clarence played louder and louder. He even tried the original Stones version but fuzzyhead refused to respond.

Finally he shoved her and she sat up, startled and annoyed. She groped for her glasses on the floor and put them on.

"I'm here to show you your future," Clarence said. "It's *Airplane II* meets *Belle de Jour* and it's rated X for exhausting."

"How'd you get in here? I'm going to call the police," Olivia said, bunching the covers up around herself.

"Did Scrooge threaten the Ghost of Christmas Past with the cops?" Clarence said, annoyed.

Olivia sat up. "Listen, Lenny—"

"My name isn't Lenny," he interrupted her. "Now, follow me."

"But I have to put in my contact lenses."

"Just wear your glasses. We don't have time."

"I'm not going anywhere in these hideous glasses," Olivia said. "And my hair is a mess. I have to blow-dry my hair."

"No one's going to see you. You're going to be invisible," Clarence said, frustrated.

"Invisible or not, I don't wear my glasses in public," Olivia insisted.

She grabbed her makeup case and Clarence waited while she went to the bathroom to put in her daily disposables. First she brushed her teeth and looked at herself in the mirror. Her hair was like a giant bush on her head. What did he mean, show her her future? She was sure she was dreaming. This was obviously just some sort of guilt dream about the fact that she hadn't told anyone that she had gotten into Princeton, Columbia, MIT, and the University of Pennsylvania and was still planning to go to U of W with her friends. She and Bill had both applied to all those schools but Bill had only been accepted at U Penn. Olivia didn't want him to feel bad, and she certainly didn't want her friends to know that the chair of the biology department at Princeton had called her personally to make her an offer. She could go to Princeton for free, with guaranteed access to labs in the medical school for her research. Ugh. The last thing Olivia wanted was for people to think she was some sort of science geek. There was definitely nothing cool about that.

She would still have to do something with her hair, even if it was only a dream. But first, her contacts. She peeled open a contact lens package and placed it carefully in her eye.

Clarence was getting agitated. He went to the bathroom door and knocked.

"Just a minute," Olivia said.

Clarence looked at his watch. He couldn't wait any longer. This was definitely going to throw off their ETA. "Your future isn't going to wait around for you to be ready," he said through the door. He strummed Olivia's chord on his guitar and they were off.

⟨19⟩

(Chicken Thumbs)

Olivia wrapped her arms tightly around Clarence's waist as they sped along on his bike. Just when she was beginning to relax, the bike left the ground and rose into the air. She opened her mouth to scream but the impulse left her. This was actually fun, and it was definitely cool.

The bike raced along in the sky until it caught up with an airplane, a 747 wide-body. They pulled up to one of the oval windows in coach and Clarence told Olivia to take a look.

She squinted a little since she was only wearing one contact lens and looked inside.

She watched a couple of balding middle-aged businessmen sitting uncomfortably in their seats. The one in the window seat was wearing a sleep mask and his cheek was pressed against the thick plastic window. A string of drool dripped from the corner of his mouth. The one in the aisle seat was reading the paper. He absent-mindedly slipped his hand into his pants.

"Don't tell me these men have anything to do with my future," Olivia said, horrified.

"In a way they do," Clarence said.

A stewardess in a navy blue uniform pushed the food cart up the aisle. The sleeping businessman snapped to attention, somehow sensing the arrival of his dinner.

"Chicken thumbs or rack of lamb?" the stewardess said to the people in the row in front of the businessmen. "All right. Rack of lamb. Enjoy. Your lamb, madam. Enjoy."

She pushed the cart forward. "Would you care to join us for some chicken thumbs this evening?" the stewardess said to the two businessmen.

"I'll take the rack of lamb," the man in the window seat said.

"I'm afraid we're out of the rack of lamb. Would you care for the chicken thumbs?"

The man grunted and she put the tray down in front of him. "I really had my little old heart set on the rack of lamb," he said, staring at the stewardess's chest. "That's a really nice rack you've got right there."

The stewardess ignored him. "Would you care to join us for some chicken thumbs tonight?" she said to the man on the aisle.

Suddenly Olivia had a horrible realization. The stewardess was *her*.

"I'm a stewardess?" she asked Clarence in disbelief.

"A *flight attendant*," he corrected.

But Olivia had the third highest grades in her school. She could have won a Westinghouse prize if she had sent in her application and not just helped Bill with his. What was she doing serving up chicken thumbs to these idiots? What the hell were chicken thumbs, anyway?

"You wanted to travel," Clarence explained. "You wanted a job with a little sex appeal. You thought it would be really cool to live with three other girls in a New York City apartment and travel the world."

"Well, that doesn't sound too bad. At least I live in New York," Olivia said.

"Uh, actually the New York City thing didn't work out. You live in St. Louis and you only travel between the St. Louis hub and Los Angeles and Madison."

"Well, at least my hair is straight."

"Straight, but if you look closely you'll see that the ends are extremely damaged."

"Hey, babe," the man on the aisle said to Olivia, who was walking by collecting empty plastic cups and trays. "You think you could rustle me up another dinner?"

"I'm afraid we're all out, sir," Olivia told him.

"But I'm still hungry."

"I'll see what I can do," Olivia said with a tired smile.

She walked to the galley and drew the curtain closed behind her. She poured herself a diet Coke. "How are you doing?" another flight attendant asked her. She was a pretty girl with a blond ponytail.

"Not too good, Courtney. I tried to get tomorrow off so I could go to my ten-year high school reunion but no one would switch with me," Olivia said.

"Wow. I just graduated high school last year. I can't even imagine going to my ten-year reunion," Courtney said. She started scraping half-eaten dinners into a garbage bag.

"Yeah, I know what you mean," Olivia said.

"I'm working tomorrow or I'd switch with you," Courtney said.

"The bozo in 27C wants another dinner," Olivia said.

Courtney picked up a tray. "Well, this one has hardly been touched, except for this one chicken thumb that looks like it was spit out."

Olivia took the slightly used tray to the man in the aisle but was stopped by a woman with a baby on her lap and her six-year-old son sprawled out next to her. The deck of playing cards that Olivia had spent twenty minutes looking for was scattered on the floor under his feet. "You wouldn't mind taking this, would you?" the mother said, handing her a bulging barf bag. "Oh, and could you take this, too?" she asked, with a meek smile.

"My hands are a little full here," Olivia said.

The woman put the balled-up poopie disposable diaper on the dinner tray that Olivia was holding in her other hand. Olivia managed to transfer the used diaper into the hand holding the barf bag and balanced the tray in her other hand.

She brought the tray to the man.

"Thanks, honey," he said, and slapped her ass. The slap startled her and she dropped the barf bag. It poured out on the man's lap.

"Goddammit," the man screamed at her. "You stupid klutz."

"I'm sorry, sir," Olivia said. "I'll get you some napkins."

"Napkins aren't going to save this suit. I have a meeting," the man screamed. He grabbed the diaper from her, not realizing what it was, and began to mop up the mess with it. The diaper's contents spilled out on his round stomach and mixed with the vomit.

"I suppose you won't be wanting the chicken thumbs now," Olivia said.

Back in the galley, Olivia and Courtney had a good laugh. But the Olivia sitting behind Clarence on his bike wasn't very amused.

"This is a nightmare," she said miserably.

Clarence wasn't really paying attention. He was watching the in-flight movie, *Harry Potter 10*.

"How's Bill?" Courtney asked Olivia.

"I don't know. He's in the lab so much I hardly ever see him," Olivia said. "His work's going really well but it doesn't pay anything and he's working so hard to get this grant. . . ." Olivia started to cry. "He just never wants to do anything." Courtney gave her a hug.

"I'm married to Bill?" the younger Olivia asked Clarence.

"What? Oh yeah. You are. He does research for a plant in St. Louis, something to do with pigs' cells and premature baldness."

Olivia pulled herself together, thanked Courtney, and headed toward the cockpit with a pot of coffee. She opened the door to the cockpit and Captain Lawrence winked at her and excused himself to go to the bathroom.

"Hi, baby," the copilot said.

"Hi, baby," she said back. Still holding the coffeepot, she put her arms around him and they kissed.

"I had a lot of fun with you in that storage closet at LAX," he said.

"Me too, RJ," Olivia said. She put the pot of coffee down and rubbed his shoulders for a few minutes.

"That's one of the things I like so much about you," RJ said. "You're good in small, cramped spaces. The cockpit, the lavatory, a storage closet . . ."

"Is that what I have to look forward to?" Olivia asked Clarence. "Just one seedy storage closet after another? I've seen enough. Please take me back."

"All right, all right. Fasten your seat belt. We may be experiencing some turbulence. This is your captain, Clarence Terence—"

Olivia interrupted him. "You know, you're really not very funny."

Clarence headed back to Earth, singing a spirited version of "I'm Leaving on a Jet Plane." He wasn't going to let these cranky teenagers rain on his groove.

A moment later Olivia was sound asleep next to Min again.

(Rated PG for Pretty Grim)

The inflatable bed felt suddenly cold for some reason and Min shuddered and sat up. The events of the night came rushing back to her. She had fought with Tobias. He had acted like a jerk at the prom. But she wished she were lying in bed with him instead of with Olivia.

Soon she would be going to the University of Wisconsin and she could spend every night with Tobias. They could live together and cook and read the papers like married people. She couldn't wait.

Maybe he had called. She got out of bed and put on her pink terry-cloth bathrobe with the dogs all over it that Tobias had given her for Valentine's Day. At first she had been disappointed because it seemed kind of like an old lady present, like something her grandfather might get for her grandmother. It wasn't exactly sexy lingerie. But she knew he had probably spent a long time picking it out and choosing the card, which he signed, *Love, Tobias and Ozzy*, so she pretended to really love it.

On her way to check the answering machine in her bedroom, she decided to stop and get something to eat in the kitchen. She was suddenly starving, despite having eaten three giant *M* pancakes and half of an *S*.

She was surprised to find the Lenny Kravitz look-alike sitting in her kitchen, helping himself to a giant corned beef sandwich.

"Where'd you get this fabulous corned beef?" he asked.

"Excuse me, what are you doing here?" Min asked him.

"I haven't had a corned beef sandwich this good since I went to temple in Brooklyn with my cousin Ben."

"You're Jewish?" Min asked.

"I'm half Jewish. I can make the best matzo ball soup you ever had. The trick is seltzer water. It makes the matzo balls as light and fluffy as clouds."

"Well, maybe you can come to our next seder and bring your soup," Min said sarcastically.

He actually looked kind of cute with mustard dripping out of the corners of his mouth.

"There's a sandwich named after me at a famous Jewish deli in New York City," Clarence said.

"Well, that's just great," Min said. "As a matter of fact, the corned beef you're stuffing your face with right now is from New York. A member of my father's synagogue brought it back for him specially, and he's going to be extremely mad when he finds it's missing tomorrow."

"He'll be even madder to find this gone," Clarence said, unwrapping a giant dill pickle from its wax paper and taking a bite.

"Do you mind telling me what you're doing in my kitchen, anyway?" Min said.

"I'm here to show you your future and have a little snack." Clarence climbed up on his kitchen stool and felt the soil of a hanging plant. He climbed back down, held a glass under the faucet, and climbed back up to water it.

"Thank you," Min said. "Wait, what am I thanking you for? You break into my house and steal my food and say you're going to show me my future?" She picked up half of his sandwich and took a huge bite. "Are you trying to tell me I'm going to be fat?" she said with her mouth full. She took another huge bite. "Ha!"

"Did Dorothy laugh in the face of Glenda the Good Witch of the North?" Clarence said. "I'm doing you a favor. I'm taking you to your own private drive-in movie theater. Tonight's feature is like *National Lampoon's Vacation* meets *Who's Afraid of Virginia Woolf?* And it's rated PG for pretty grim."

"Well, it will have to wait until I check my answering machine," Min said.

Clarence didn't wait for Min to check her machine. He picked up his guitar from the kitchen stool next to him and played Min's song, "Love the One You're With," by Crosby, Stills & Nash.

Suddenly his black shades lit up and Min became entranced. It was like she was watching a videotape in fast forward. She saw herself as a tiny infant being held high above her father's head as he walked on a beach, being fed in a high chair, her first steps. The tape sped up. Her first day at school, learning to read, smiling with missing teeth. Faster and faster it got until it was just a blur. And then it stopped in a freeze-frame.

"Here's the good part," Clarence said. And suddenly Min and Clarence were *inside* the frame.

Tobias sat cross-legged on a sandy beach, with a drum in front of him, holding Ozzy on his lap. He was in a circle with six other men. All the men had drums in front of them.

"Tobias," Min called. "Tobias! Ozzy!"

"They can't hear you," Clarence said. "And besides, you're not welcome here. This is the men's empowerment meeting. It's men only."

"What the hell are you talking about?" Min asked.

The men all started banging on their drums. It sounded terrible but they were really getting into it. Ozzy slunk off down the beach and put his paws over his ears. Tobias banged his drum the loudest.

Clarence grabbed a drum that was lying in the sand and banged along with them. He looked a little silly because his drum was a lot smaller than all the other drums, which was why no one else had chosen it. He was also the only one in full biker/rock star regalia. The other men were wearing very little clothing. One guy was wearing only a loincloth made of hemp. Tobias was wearing his black Bulls shorts, without any shirt. He had a huge hairy belly. The top of his head was sunburned where his hair had thinned.

"We are brothers!" the leader yelled, standing in the middle of the circle and waving a big shaky stick. He was a skinny little man with a bushy beard, wearing pink cut-off shorts and a pink tank top. The shaky stick was bigger than both his skinny legs put together.

"We are brothers!" the men yelled back.

"We are strong!"

"We are strong!"

"We are hunters. We are builders. We're providers. We are men!"

The men repeated the drill.

"Our wives don't tell us what to do!"

Tobias suddenly looked like he was remembering something, like a cartoon character with a lightbulb over his head. He stopped drumming and looked at his watch.

"I have to go," he told the group leader. "I have couple's therapy with my wife now in the Rose Room."

"It's important for you to take time for yourself," the group leader said. "You have to be a man."

"Yeah, yeah," Tobias said, "but I'll be a man with no dick after my wife chops it off and blends it into a smoothie if I miss couple's therapy."

"Would you please tell me what's going on?" Min asked Clarence. "Where are we?"

"It's a couples' retreat in Baja, California," Clarence said. "A sort of Club Med for the dysfunctional. A romantic hideaway for those heading for divorce. A weekend for those wedded in holy misery."

"What does that have to do with banging on a drum?" Min asked.

"Look, I don't write this stuff," Clarence said. "All I know is your marriage is like that piece of driftwood over there." He pointed at a rotting old log on the beach that Ozzy was taking a long piss on.

Min remembered that she had a little trick for when she was having a bad dream. She could force herself to wake up. "Good-bye, Lenny," she said to Clarence, and shut her eyes tight. Then she opened them again but Clarence was still there.

"My name is not Lenny," he said. "Meet your therapist, Miss White."

Min looked at the woman sitting in the armchair wearing a khaki skort and a green plastic visor even though they were inside. "Congratulations on coming to Marriage Minded and taking the first step toward healing your relationship," Miss White said.

"Now meet yourself," Clarence said.

Min gasped. She saw herself sitting on a love seat next to Tobias, her *husband,* with Ozzy sitting between them. She didn't look good. She was *fat,* and Tobias was fat and balding. Even Ozzy was fat and balding. He had lost most of his fur due to a psychosomatic dog skin disease caused by the fights between Min and Tobias.

"Who wants to begin?" Miss White asked.

For a moment nobody spoke. Then the future Min began to cry. "It's hopeless," she said. "We've been together since high school and it's just not working anymore. Tomorrow is my ten-year high school reunion and I really wanted to go but I didn't want everyone to see us like this."

"Who cares about your stupid reunion," Tobias said.

"That's the same thing you said about my senior prom," Min yelled.

Ozzy whimpered and scratched at himself.

"You drag me all the way to this nuthouse funny farm to talk about the prom!" Tobias yelled. "We could have done this at home."

"Well, that's exactly where I'm going," Min said. "Home."

"I would strongly recommend that you stay and take the couples' massage class tonight at six-thirty in the Blue Room," Miss White said.

"I'm not good at massage," Tobias said, caressing Ozzy and kneading him in his favorite spot, just above the tail.

"You seem to give your dog a lot of affection," Miss White commented. "If you don't want to do couples' massage, perhaps you would consider going on the couples' cruise later tonight."

"Ozzy gets seasick," Tobias said.

Min thundered back to the bungalow with Tobias and Ozzy following. She threw her things in her suitcase, including the ratty old dog bathrobe.

Clarence thumbed through the room service menu

while the younger and still relatively thin Min watched herself in a state of shock.

"Isn't this what you wanted?" Clarence asked Min.

"To be fat and miserable? I don't think so." But she knew he was right. The only future she had ever really imagined for herself was being married to Tobias. It had never occurred to her that things could turn out like this.

"You're not leaving me in this loony bin," Tobias said. "We're going with you."

"I don't care what you do," Min snapped. She was still crying.

"Well, you should care. You're my wife and you better start acting like it."

Min grabbed her suitcase and dragged it off the bed and out the door.

Tobias waddled after Min through LAX. They were wearing matching nylon running suits and Ozzy, who was nestled happily in Tobias's carry-on bag, was wearing a matching running suit, too.

They stopped at the airport Pizza Hut stand and silently ate two deep-dish pizzas, gingerly feeding some of their pepperoni to Ozzy.

Clarence perused the racks of paperback books in the airport souvenir store. "Can you believe the crap people read today?" he asked Min. "And look at this shit." He pointed to the snow domes that said

Hollywood and Disneyland on them, the shot glasses, the Marilyn Monroe ashtrays. One whole shelf was filled with gold plastic replicas of Oscars, with Best Friend, Best Secretary, Best Actor, Best Lawyer stamped on them. He picked up one that said Best Wife on it and handed it to Min.

"That's not funny," she said.

Min and Tobias had barely spoken on the flight from Baja to LA and when their flight to Madison was called they got up without speaking and went to the gate. Clarence and Min rode beside them on an airport go-cart.

Olivia stood just inside the door of the plane, greeting the travelers. A fat couple approached. "We'll be needing the seat belt extenders," she whispered to another flight attendant. She looked down at the names printed on the tickets. Frank, Min. Frank, Tobias.

"Min?" she said in disbelief.

"Olivia?" Min said, clutching her stomach in surprise.

Suddenly the curtain separating first class opened and Claudia Choney emerged. "Hi!" she said. "Oh, my, is that Olivia? A stewardess! I'm sorry, you girls like to be called flight attendants now, don't you? And is that Min? Big with child! You must be in your ninth month. I didn't even know they let you fly when you're that pregnant."

Just then Ozzy jumped out of Tobias's carry-on bag and started humping Claudia's leg.

"Please, please take me home," Min begged Clarence. "I can't stand to watch this anymore."

"It's not exactly my favorite episode of *Fantasy Island,* either," Clarence said, tucking a little airline bottle of scotch in his pocket. "Come on, let's go."

The next thing Min knew she was throwing up half a corned beef sandwich in her very own bathroom back home. She looked at herself in the mirror, checking to make sure she still had only one chin, and ran her hands all over her body. What a terrible, terrible dream. No more champagne before bed, she decided, and crawled back onto the air mattress, next to Olivia.

(Rated G for Get a Life)

Now only Sally was left, Clarence thought. At least her future was local and didn't involve another time zone. All the flying was making Clarence puffy and bloated and he was happy to give it a rest for a little while. He was feeling stressed out again and would be glad to call it a night.

But Sally was different from the other three girls. She would understand the importance of what he was trying to do for her. She would think about it, struggle to make sense of the whole thing, try to write about it in that diary of hers. Of course, since there could be no real record of the future, anything she wrote about it would disappear the minute the ink hit paper, as if she were writing with an invisible pen.

Clarence went down to the rumpus room but Sally wasn't in bed. She was gone. Then he saw her sound asleep on the floor next to the sofa bed. She couldn't sleep with Zola lying so close, so, sadly, she had put her pillow on the floor.

Clarence sat down on the floor next to her and stroked the top of her head. "Sally. Sally," he whispered.

Sally woke up, terrified that it was Zola touching her. Instead of being scared out of her mind to see a gorgeous black guy with a guitar, she was actually relieved.

"Lenny!" she said.

"My name isn't Lenny, it's Clarence Terence."

"I remember, Clarence," she said, becoming flushed. Had Lenny broken into the Weinstocks' basement just to see her? She had definitely felt a connection between them but she hadn't realized it was mutual. That's how she had always heard it was supposed to be. Two people saw each other, felt something, a spark, and they just knew it was right. She couldn't believe he had chosen her over the others. Thank God she hadn't wasted her time with that immature Dean Merren or that moronic Jason Altman.

Lenny was who she'd been waiting for all along. A real man. A musician. She was stupid to have thought she could ever get along with a high school boy. She couldn't wait to ride with Lenny on the back of his motorcycle. And introduce him to her mother. Her mother would have a complete freak-out when she saw him. And Lenny would be understanding about the fact that she was a virgin. They understood each other.

"Oh, Clarence." She sighed. She closed her eyes and leaned into him.

"Sally, are you okay? You're all red," Clarence said worriedly.

"Clarence, I . . ." Sally leaned forward to kiss him. She got up on her knees, put her arms around his neck, and kissed him hard on the lips.

Clarence was even more shocked than Sally had been when Zola had kissed her. He pushed her away.

"Damn, girl, did George Bailey in *It's a Wonderful Life* try to rape the angel who showed him his future and saved his life? I'm your fairy godmother, not your lover, baby."

Sally was mortified. She had never felt so humiliated in her entire life, and that was really saying something since she was always humiliating herself one way or another. "What are you talking about?" she said. She felt like crying. Why hadn't he wanted to kiss her? What had she done wrong? He probably liked one of the other girls better and he just wanted to talk to her to find out how he could get her to like him. Boys were always coming up to her and asking what they should do to get Zola to go out with them. "What are you doing here?" she demanded.

"I'm here to show you your future. And I didn't expect you to plant one on me like that."

"My future?" Sally asked. "What do you mean, show me my future?"

"It's sort of like *Mary Poppins* meets *The Sound of Music* and it's rated G for get a life."

Sally's heart fell. It would figure she'd be wearing Min's stupid oversized Minnie Mouse Disney T-shirt at a moment like this.

"Who are you to tell me to get a life?" Sally said, surprising herself. "You're the one going to other people's proms, sneaking around people's basements and putting your nose where it doesn't belong. That's pretty pathetic, if you ask me. What do you care about my future?"

Clarence felt like giving up. What the hell was wrong with these people? He sulked for a minute and then remembered that line about seeing discouragement as opportunity, from *The Buddha at Work*. The rock of greater good was sitting somewhere on the horizon. To get there he would have to turn this boat around.

"Look, Sally baby . . ."

"I'm not your baby," Sally said. She was on a roll. "You know, you really have a lot of nerve coming in here and leading me on like that and saying my life was going to be like a Walt Disney musical." She held her pillow in front of her, trying to hide the Minnie Mouse T-shirt. "My life is not a movie. It's real. It isn't anything meets anything. My future has nothing to do with an ex-nun in Austria who becomes a nanny or a nanny who flies around with a parasol. And what's with this obsession with Julie Andrews, anyway?"

"I am not obsessed with Julie Andrews!" Clarence said. "Let me just show you your future and then we can call it a night."

"No," Sally said. "I don't want to see it. Why don't you just go rent *Victor/Victoria* and leave me alone?"

"What do you mean, you don't want to see it?" Clarence said, frustrated beyond belief. He had never heard of anyone not wanting to see their future. Who wouldn't jump at the chance to see how his or her life would turn out? Why was Sally acting like this? It was almost as if she was afraid of something. Zola stretched and turned over on the sofa bed. Sally clutched the pillow tighter, shying away from Zola. Of course, that was it. Sally was afraid she might turn out to be a lesbian.

Sally looked so cute, holding her pillow like that and staring at him with her big frightened blue eyes. Clarence was suddenly filled with fatherly love for her. It was a hard thing to be a seventeen-year-old girl, facing her future. Of course she was scared. He should be more sensitive, Clarence scolded himself.

"Sally, I'm sorry," he said gently. "I think we got off on the wrong foot. I'm only trying to help. If you don't want to see your future, I'm not going to force you. *Que sera sera,* whatever will be will be, the future's not ours to see, and all that."

Sally cocked her head and looked at him. "Will I be a writer?" she asked him.

"Oh no," Clarence said. "You said you didn't want to see your future and you're not going to see it."

"Just tell me if I'm a writer," Sally said.

"I'm sorry," Clarence said. "I promised I wouldn't show you your future and I'm going to hold myself to that. But I'll tell you one thing, Sally." He stroked her cheek tenderly. "You're a good person. And you really deserve the best. And I for one will definitely be keeping an eye out for you. I would never let anything bad happen to you. Not to you, or Min, or Olivia, or Zola."

Sally suddenly felt incredibly safe.

"So that's what it's like to have a fairy godmother?" she asked. "Like in the movie *Grease* when Frankie Avalon comes down and sings 'Beauty School Dropout'?"

"That's it *exactly*, Sally," Clarence said. "Now I know we really understand each other."

"I'll tell you what," Sally said. "I'll let you show me my future if you let me call you Lenny."

"All right." Clarence sighed. "Whatever floats your boat." He picked up his guitar and began to play Sally's theme, "You're Lost, Little Girl," by The Doors.

Bravely Sally closed her eyes and screwed up her whole face, ready for whatever lay ahead of her. "I'm ready, Lenny," she said.

㉑

⟮Go Back to High School⟯

"What are you doing?" Clarence asked. With her eyes closed like that, Sally looked like she was getting ready to blast off into outer space.

Sally opened her eyes. "I figured you were going to zap us someplace," she said. "Zap us into the future."

"Actually, I thought we'd walk."

"Oh," Sally said, a little disappointed. She had the kind of future you could walk to. So much for her dream of living in Paris or Rome.

Sally and Clarence walked along the quiet streets of Madison until she found herself standing in front of old La Follette High.

"What are we doing here, Lenny?"

"Just taking you to the prom," he said.

"I thought you were taking me into the future, not the past," Sally said. She had dreamed about the prom for so long, it was weird to think that it was already over, already in the past.

The gym was cast in a bright red glow. Brightly colored Styrofoam balls that looked like planets and figures cut out of oak tag that looked like Martians with giant lightbulb-shaped heads and slits for eyes hung everywhere. Kids were dancing in a strange way. Sort of waltzing. It looked futuristic and old-fashioned all at the same time. Sally had never seen these kids before. The band was new. They were called Rick's Pink Slicker. If this was the future, people were still coming up with idiotic names for bands.

"Aren't they awful?" Clarence said. "They're retro techno. The worst."

"What's going on?" Sally asked.

"It's the prom; I already told you," Clarence said. "They finally got sick of *Titanic,* thank God. The theme is alien love this year. Of course that's old news by now. It's been a year since humans made contact with beings on another planet."

Sally looked around in disbelief. "Look, it's old man Otis," she said. Otis was even older, bopping up and down in time to the music. Sally called to him but he didn't turn around.

"He can't see or hear you," Clarence said.

Otis was already starting to take down some of the

decorations even though the prom wasn't over yet. Miss McCormack went over to help him in her Easy Spirit shoes along with another woman Sally didn't recognize. How terrible to be a grown woman and have to go back to the prom year after year. By now Miss McCormack was probably addicted to snorting baby powder. "Why are they doing that?" Sally asked.

"Doing what?" Clarence asked. He was helping himself to a generous cup of punch that was turning his lips and tongue blue. "Oh, you mean taking down the decorations? They're probably getting ready for tomorrow's reunion. They had to schedule them back-to-back. It's *your* reunion, as a matter of fact. Your ten-year reunion."

"So then I guess we're early," Sally said. "We got here a day too soon. This prom has nothing to do with me."

Sally was interrupted by a girl wearing dumb googly antennae going up onstage and introducing the new homecoming king and queen.

"Hey, that's Zola's little brother, Nathaniel." Sally giggled. "Wow, he's gorgeous."

Nathaniel Mitchell, wearing his new crown at a jaunty angle, approached the microphone. "Uh, on behalf of our whole senior class we just wanted to thank a teacher who has meant a lot to us over the last four years."

Sally snickered to herself. She hated teachers who tried to be all buddy-buddy with the students.

"So," Nathaniel continued, "everyone raise your glasses to a really cool teacher. Thank you, Miss Wilder."

Sally gasped and gripped Clarence's hand. She watched in horror as Miss Wilder turned from helping Otis and Miss McCormack and waved at Nathaniel and all the applauding kids. Miss Wilder was her.

"I'm a teacher?" Sally asked. She couldn't imagine anything worse. "At this stupid school? I don't even get to leave La Follette?"

"Don't be like that," Clarence said. "It's not so bad. There are a lot worse things you could be."

"Like what?" Sally asked. At that moment she really couldn't think of anything worse. Being a teacher at the same school you went to was like standing still. It was like being frozen in time. She might as well be a statue in a museum or a hamster on a wheel.

"Oh, come on. It's not like you're a bathroom attendant or a tollbooth clerk. You don't work at McDonald's or Hooters. You're not a bill collector for the Internal Revenue Service, or a prison guard, or a homeless junkie prostitute, or . . ." Clarence tried to think of the worst possible thing a person could end up being. "Or a lawyer!" he added.

"This is terrible," Sally said.

"I really think you're overreacting here, Sally. You're a good teacher and all the kids *love* you. You taught that one how to drive," he said, pointing to a geeky girl with giant glasses. "You helped that one when her parents got divorced. You chaperon all the overnight field trips. You took them all to see *The Island of La Grande Jatte,* by Georges Seurat, at the arts museum in Chicago. You try to be like a best friend to a lot of them."

Sally was getting seriously depressed. She looked over at herself waving at the kids. She had put on a little weight and she was wearing a dowdy dress but she was still her. She could still see her old self buried under there. Why couldn't she just wake up and see that things could be different? She wanted to run over and put her hands on her own shoulders and shake and shake and shake. Don't stay here, she wanted to yell. Go somewhere else. Travel. Live!

"So I'm not a writer," Sally whispered.

"You are. You write and *direct* the annual school play. And isn't that what most creative people want—*to direct?*"

Clarence felt terrible. He hadn't meant for Sally to take things this hard. He should have at least picked her up one of those plastic Best Teacher Oscars at the airport in LA. She looked like she was going to cry. Zola's little brother, who wasn't so little anymore, was dancing with his queen on the dance floor and the other kids were starting to join in.

Clarence grabbed the antenna headband off a girl's head and put it on Sally. "Would you do me the honor of giving me this dance?" he asked.

"You're such a kleptomaniac, aren't you, Lenny?" Sally sighed, adjusting the antennae on her head.

They danced to a slow song, Sally's head resting sadly on Clarence's chest. She felt a little silly dancing in Min's Minnie Mouse T-shirt and wearing antennae while everyone else was wearing tuxes and gowns. She looked over at herself. "Miss Wilder" was now sitting on the bleachers. She took a diary out of her shoulder bag and began to write in it. Probably writing about the kids giving her a big round of applause, Sally figured. Probably writing about how, just ten years before, she was at her own prom with Min, Olivia, and Zola. Probably writing with eager anticipation about her ten-year reunion tomorrow. It was so sad.

"At least I better have a great house," Sally said to Clarence. "And a great boyfriend."

"Well . . ." Clarence didn't want to give her any more bad news.

"Spit it out," Sally said.

"You still live at home with your mother," Clarence mumbled, trying to cover his mouth with his hand.

"What?" Sally asked. She hoped she hadn't heard the word *mother*.

"You still live at home with your mother. And you've never had a real boyfriend. You're still a virgin, Sally."

"Noooooooooo!" Sally screamed.

"Sally, wake up," Zola said, shaking her. Sally sat up. She was back on Min's sofa bed.

"You were having a bad dream," Olivia said.

Sally looked around the rumpus room. Lenny was gone. Her friends were there. They were still seventeen. It was just a bad dream, she told herself. Just a little nightmare.

(The Dominant Male Figure)

"That was the worst dream I've ever had," Sally told the other girls.

"Me too," Olivia, Min, and Zola said at the exact same time.

"I was so gross," Zola said when she had told them every sordid detail. "Claudia Choney had everything. She was married to Evan and they had a beautiful daughter, and I had nothing, not even a driver's license. I really hate her."

"I was just such a ditz," Olivia said after telling them about her mile-high misery. "I had no self-respect whatsoever."

"At least you and Zola had jobs," Min said, after telling them about her fabulous marriage to Tobias. "I was married to a man who loved a bald dog more than me." She took off her doggy bathrobe, crumpled it into an angry ball, and threw it across the room.

150

"I think we can all agree that you had it great compared to me," Sally said. "I never even left La Follette! And I was still a virgin! Just thinking about it makes me feel insane."

"What did your father put in those pancakes, Min?" Zola asked.

"Well, it was only a dream," Min said, as if she was trying to convince herself. "You're smart, Olivia. Why'd we all dream about the future?"

"Yeah," Zola said. "I'm sure there's a very logical explanation for why we dreamed the things we did. I mean when you think about it, it makes sense. We're at a point in our lives when we're thinking a lot about the future. High school is almost over. And we drank all that champagne."

"But that doesn't explain why that biker dude was in *all* of our dreams," Olivia countered.

"Well, there's a reasonable explanation for that, too," Zola continued. "I had Mrs. Williams last semester for English and you know how she is so obsessed with psychology, well, she told us all about Jungian dream analysis. In our dreams everything symbolizes something. We all saw that Clarence freak riding on his kick-ass motorcycle and he represented the dominant male figure in our psyches. I mean, it's really obvious. Sally said there were Martians in her dream. The theme of the prom in her dream had to do with outer space. And look, she's wearing that stupid antenna headband." Zola pointed to the top of Sally's head. "So she put on that headband before she went to sleep and that's why she had that dream."

Sally slowly moved her hand to the top of her head and removed the antennae. She looked at them with her eyes as wide as flying saucers. "I . . . I . . ." How could she tell them she had never seen them before the dream?

"Yeah, Zola's right," Olivia said. She got up but the room looked so strange and blurry she sat back down.

"You're hungover," Min said.

"Yeah, I guess I am," Olivia said. Then she realized she was wearing one contact lens. "That's weird. I could have sworn I took out my contacts last night."

"You did," Sally said. "Remember? You put on your glasses and made a big deal about telling Rabbi Weinstock not to take your picture in them?"

"That's right," Olivia said, confused.

Min noticed something poking out of the covers on the air mattress. "What's this?" she said, pulling out the Oscar statuette for Best Wife.

"Okay, Zola," Min whispered. "Are you going to tell us I just happened to have this thing lying around the house? Yeah, I always take my Best Wife Oscar thingy to bed with me."

Zola was silent.

Min was getting sort of hysterical. She jumped up on the sofa bed and held the Oscar high up in the air. "I'd like to thank the Academy and Mr. Clarence Terence, whoever you are, for presenting me with this Worst Future award."

"There must be an explanation," Zola said.

"Okay, Dr. Freud," Sally said to Zola. "Then how do you explain *that?*"

"What?" Zola asked.

Sally pointed at Zola and Zola brought her hand up to her throat. There, around Zola's neck, were her mother's pearls, all put back together again.

Clarence Terence knew a good jeweler in Manhattan's diamond district who had agreed to do a rush job on the pearls. But he'd forgotten to buy more corned beef while he was in New York.

"Girls!" Rabbi Weinstock yelled angrily, knocking on the door to the basement. "Who raided my fridge last night?" he shouted.

Clarence cringed. Oh, well. He couldn't think of everything. He was only a fairy godmother. He never said he was perfect. At least he didn't implement some of the more dramatic devices. He didn't have things turn into pumpkins at the stroke of midnight like *some* people. He tried to keep things real.

And he was particularly proud of the restrung pearls

touch. He hoped Zola would see it as a symbol for the future, since she was apparently so into symbolism. He hoped all the girls would see that if something fell apart, you could pick up all the pieces and put them together again in a slightly different way. It might not be exactly the same, but it might be better.

He had done his job and shown them their futures. He just hoped they would figure out that if they changed things around *now,* their lives would look a lot different *then*. Or was it if they changed their lives *then,* speaking from the future, then what was *then* would be *now* and their *nows* would be different because of their *thens*. Or . . . Wait, now he was getting confused. Sometimes it got so overwhelming. All he knew was, one small change could make a big difference.

Clarence headed toward Maple Bluff on his bike. He was going to treat himself to the best suite in the best hotel, complete with room service, a massage, a big white fluffy robe, and chocolate pillow mints. If he had to hang around Earth he might as well indulge in some earthly delights now and then.

(23)

(A Very Deep Promise)

"So what are we going to do?" Sally asked the other girls. "We can't just go on knowing what we know and not do anything about it."

"Sally's right," Zola said. "The Four Pigs have to stick together."

"Do we still have to call ourselves the Four Pigs?" Olivia asked. "I don't think it's the most flattering name we could come up with."

"How about the Four Future Freaks?" Zola suggested.

"Okay, the Four Pigs is fine," Olivia said.

"I'm going to go on a big diet," Min said, remembering how fat she was in her future.

"It can't be anything that superficial, Min," Zola said.

"That's easy for you to say, Zola. Miss Thin Nudie Model. Some of us have to watch our weight."

"Fine, Min," Zola said. "But I think we need to change something more profound. Something *symbolic*."

"We each have to make a very deep promise," Sally said.

"Wait here," Min said. "I have to go upstairs and get something."

She ran all the way up to the attic, not even stopping to check her machine. In a box with her old roller skates—skates, not blades—she found the Four Pigs' shoe box with the old diet Coke in it. She brought it back down to the girls.

They sat in a circle on the floor.

Zola went first. With her hand touching the pearls around her neck she made her vow. "I, Zola Mitchell, promise to get *even*," she said solemnly.

"Get even or get Evan?" Min asked.

"Both. And I'm not joking around," Zola said. "I'm going to get even with Claudia Choney and get Evan, too." By the time she finished with Claudia and had Evan back there was no way her future would turn out the same.

"I have something to tell you guys," Olivia said, looking down at the blanket on the sofa bed. "I did a little better on my SATs than I said. I got into MIT."

Olivia saw the girls all glance at each other. "We know, Olivia," Zola said. "The science teachers have been bragging about it. Everyone kind of knows."

Olivia couldn't believe they had known all along when

she tried her best to keep it a secret. But none of that mattered anymore. "Well, I think I should seriously consider going. From now on I'm going to study and work hard so I don't end up president of the Mile-High Club," she vowed. She took the contact lens out of her eye and put on her glasses. "From now on it's geeky Old Four Eyes," she said. "I don't care what anyone says."

Min clutched her Best Wife Oscar to her chest. "I'm going to break up with Tobias," she announced.

"And Ozzy," Zola prompted.

"And Ozzy," Min said. "I'm going to fly into my future solo. My own woman. I need a man who respects me. Even though I'll really miss them," she added softly.

Then Zola, Olivia, and Min all looked at Sally.

"What are you going to do?" Zola asked.

Sally put her Martian antennae on her head and with one hand on her diary and one hand in the air, she made her vow. "I, Sally Wilder, solemnly swear to *get laid!*" If she had sex now there was no way she'd wind up a virgin teacher living with her mother. She could join the ranks of the great, gifted lover/writers she idolized. "Get ready," she whooped. "Here I come!"

"Shhh," Min said, "my parents are right upstairs."

"I don't care who knows it," Sally said. "I vow to not be a virgin by graduation. No matter how and no matter who, I am going to have sex. With a man," she added.

"Of course with a man; doesn't that go without saying?" Min asked.

Min cracked open the old warm can of diet Coke and took a sip. She made a face. "I didn't know diet Coke could go bad."

They passed the can around and each girl took a vile sip. Then they put an unopened bottle of Taittinger's in the shoe box, put the lid on, and each held a side of the box.

"We'll drink the champagne together at our ten-year reunion," Zola said. "And we'll compare our lives then."

"Now. Let's get to work," Olivia said.

"And I know the perfect place to begin," Min said. "The prom breakfast!"

The girls all hugged, even Zola and Sally, and went to their separate homes to shower and change and get ready for the prom breakfast in the school cafeteria. Min went into the kitchen to face her father. She couldn't very well tell him that a half-Jewish black fairy godmother from another planet had eaten his corned beef. She had no choice but to take the blame.

(Get Serious)

When Olivia arrived at her house her mother was meditating on the living-room floor. She opened one eye. "Honey, your friend Bill came by and brought you something," she said.

"Who? Bill Buchanan from school?" Olivia asked.

"I'm not sure. That sounds right."

"What is it?" Olivia asked. She couldn't believe Bill would come by and bring her something. He had never even been to her house before.

"I made him take it out to the garage," her mother answered, keeping her eyes closed. "How was the prom?"

Olivia ignored her mother's question and rushed to the garage to see what Bill had brought her.

Olivia found herself facing the skeleton from the bio lab closet. The skeleton she and Bill had had so many intimate moments with. Bill had stolen it for her and dressed it in his tuxedo, complete with bow tie. A note was pinned to his boutonniere. *I love you down to my bones,* it said.

"He loves me?" Olivia asked the skeleton in disbelief. Bill loved her? No one had ever said that to her before. She kissed the skeleton on its skull where its lips would be if it had any. How could she get her act together, just when she was falling in love? She felt a tingle deep inside her abdomen and remembered what she and Bill had done together the night before. She remembered the way she had wrapped her legs around him. Why was she thinking about this? A serious person didn't spend her time having sex on tables in laboratories and talking to skeletons in garages.

She gave the skeleton one last kiss on the cheekbone and ran upstairs to her bedroom to get ready for the prom breakfast. She got a serious-looking plaid skirt and blue blazer out of her closet. But then she worried that the ensemble looked a little too much like a stewardess uniform. She tore through her closet, looking for something that wasn't too sexy. Everything she owned was so low cut.

Finally she came up with a black turtleneck sweater even though it was a hot June day. She showered and washed her hair, and towel dried it. She left it wet and curly and put on her glasses. Bill had never seen her in glasses. He'd never even seen her with her hair natural.

"Olivia Buchanan," she tried out loud. "No, stop," she said, looking through a pile of papers for that MIT acceptance letter.

23¾

(All New Underwear)

Back in her own room, Sally sat on her bed under her Lenny Kravitz poster and wrote in her diary. *Well, you're not going to believe this one,* she wrote. She wrote as fast as she could, describing what a hideous sight Lenny had shown her. Herself. At the end of ten long pages she was exhausted. She didn't even know why she was bothering to write it all down. It wasn't like she was ever going to forget it. As long as she lived, she would always remember every second of that night.

She closed the book and lay back on her bed. With everything that had happened to her in the last twenty-four hours, you'd think there'd be a lot on her mind, but all she could really think about was underwear. If she was going to lose her virginity at any moment she would need all new underwear. Maybe she'd get the ones with the days of the week printed on them and try to get devirginized by the time Wednesday or Thursday came around.

She decided to make a note of this important fact in her diary and opened it again. But when she looked down at the lined page she couldn't write; her hands were shaking too badly. Her ten pages of writing had vanished. All that remained was the first sentence she had written, and the last.

Well, you're not going to believe this one. And, *That is why we are going to the prom breakfast, because it seems like the perfect place to start.*

Sally was beginning to think her future was probably going to include a long stay at the Wisconsin State loony bin.

(24)

(Matzo Ball Soup)

Just as he was getting comfortable in a freshly turned down king-size bed with a goose down feather bed underneath him and a goose down comforter above, Clarence thought of Zola and he realized there was something he had forgotten to tell her. In fact, there were things he had forgotten to tell all the girls. He was so annoyed he could quack. He tried to convince himself it could wait until later, but how could he rest knowing the girls were probably already screwing everything up?

Clarence got dressed and opened the door to his room, taking one last longing look at the Do Not Disturb sign hanging from the doorknob uselessly.

Zola carefully took off her mother's pearls and put them in her seashell jewelry box. The jewelry box was extremely tacky but she liked it anyway. She laid the pearls out on a red velvet tray.

Clarence knocked on Zola's bedroom door.

"Come in, Mom," she said, without thinking. Then she froze. Why had she said Mom? She hoped her father or brother, or whoever had knocked, hadn't heard her. She suddenly felt like crying.

For some reason she felt incredibly relieved when it was Clarence who opened the door and came in.

"Fairy godmother, not mother," Clarence said.

"How about if I call you Fairy Mom?" Zola asked.

"I'm beginning to think I like being called Lenny," Clarence said.

Zola closed the seashell lid.

"Don't do that," Clarence said.

"Do what?"

"Put them away. You should wear them."

"No," Zola said. "I don't want to lose them."

"Your mother gave them to you to wear and you should wear them. Don't shut your memories into a dark box. It's as bad as Sally keeping her feelings buried between the covers of a diary. Here, let me help you with them."

Clarence tried to work the pearls' tiny gold clasp. He fumbled with it for a few seconds.

"I can do it," Zola said. "Don't worry." In her hands, the clasp closed easily and Zola looked in the mirror, beaming. She turned to show Clarence how she looked in them, but he was gone.

Zola picked up the phone to call Min to tell her what had happened. Rabbi Weinstock answered even though she had called Min's private line.

"You girls must have been pretty busy last night," he said.

"What do you mean?" Zola asked. She didn't think Min would have told her parents about what had happened.

Min grabbed the phone away from him. "I was just telling my dad how we stayed up all night making that *big pot of matzo ball soup* that we left on the stove as a *surprise* for him and how you knew the recipe from *home ec* last semester."

Zola had no idea what Min was talking about. She had never even eaten matzo ball soup, let alone made it.

"Zola," Steven Weinstock said into the phone. "You have to give me that recipe. It was the best soup I've ever tasted. I've never seen matzo balls so big and fluffy before."

"Uh," Zola said.

Min grabbed the phone again. "I was telling him how you said the secret ingredient was *seltzer water*," Min said. She really sounded crazy.

"Lenny was there, wasn't he?" Zola said.

"Yes, seltzer water, that's right," Min said.

"Did you see him?"

"No, it wasn't too salty," Min said.

"He was here, too," Zola said. "Let's just get to the prom breakfast before anything else happens."

"Good idea," Min said, and they hung up.

(25)

(Hair Net Betty)

Zola, Min, Sally, and Olivia arrived at La Follette High School's famous prom breakfast, only to find the cafeteria empty. Except for one table of four geeks and a few individual geeks all sitting at separate tables and Hair Net Betty, a lunch lady who not only wore a hair net but, for some unfathomable reason, also wore old, dirty Isotoner slippers.

The girls looked at the gruesome scene in complete dismay. This was hardly the setting they'd imagined for the start of their new exciting lives.

"All right, Sally, you first," Zola whispered. "You want to get laid. Now's your chance. I know it's slim pickings but you might as well go for it. Which one of these fine male specimens will be your deflowerer?" She pointed to the entire chess club—two boys with bangs so long they could barely see. "Actually, you'll be deflowering each other. Come on, Sally, beggars can't be choosers."

Sally was beginning to think it would be better to live with her mother, stay at La Follette High forever, and die an old maid than even have to talk to one of those boys.

"Well, we might as well make the best of it," Min said, grabbing an orange tray.

"What happened to your serious diet?" Olivia asked.

"I'll just have a small bowl of Cap'n Crunch with skim milk. I think it's fat free."

The other girls grabbed trays and Hair Net Betty scooped scrambled eggs onto paper plates. "Can I ask you a question?" Min asked Hair Net Betty. "Why do you wear those slippers to work? Shouldn't you keep your slippers at home by your bed, for your dog to chew?"

Hair Net Betty smiled. "You gotta have a gimmick," she said.

"I thought strippers had to have a gimmick, not lunch ladies," Olivia said.

"Whether you're a lunch lady or one of them ladies who lunch you still gotta have a gimmick," Hair Net Betty said.

"I don't know what's more surreal," Zola said, "this conversation or what happened last night."

"You girls all right?" Betty asked. "You look like you've seen a ghost."

"We're just in shock at how lame this prom breakfast is," Min said.

"Why are you surprised?" Betty asked. "I don't know

why they even bother to keep up this silly tradition. Every year only a few kids show up. Most of the kids are out all night at parties. They probably haven't even been home yet. But no one asks my opinion. I've been in this school for ten years and I'll probably be here for ten more."

Sally cringed. In ten years, Hair Net Betty would probably be her best friend and colleague.

Propelled by this thought, Sally marched over to the chess club duo. "Hi," she said to the less shaggy of the two. "Your name is Eugene, isn't it?"

"No," the boy said, with a mouth full of Cap'n Crunch.

Both boys got up and walked off with their trays, leaving Sally standing there like an idiot.

Just then a strange announcement came over the PA system. It was the principal, Mr. Seidman. "Will Min Weinstock please report to the office for a phone call?" His voice boomed through the empty cafeteria.

The four girls went to the main office together.

"Hello, Min. Hello, Zolar, Oliviar, Sally." Mr. Seidman always put an *r* sound on the end of any name that ended with an *a* sound. "The office is closed today. I was just catching up on some paperwork. But an emergency call came in for you from a Mr. Ozzy Dogman so I took a chance that you might be at the breakfast. Although I'd think you girls'd be off *partying*."

The girls suppressed a laugh. Mr. Seidman looked

ridiculous when he tried to say things like *partying*. Certain people just weren't able to carry off certain words.

Min picked up the phone. "Hello?" she said. The girls gathered around her to hear her side of the conversation.

"Where have you been?" Tobias asked. "Ozzy and I have been worried sick. Your cell phone has been out of range all night."

"That's because it's at the bottom of the lake."

"It's not funny, Min. We've been really worried. Ozzy isn't feeling well. He has terrible diarrhea. He's used up six issues of *The Onion* and all my *Isthmus Weekly*s. And I think I caught it from him," Tobias whined. "I'm sitting on the toilet right now."

"Well, I don't know what you want me to do about it. I'm having a great time at the prom breakfast with my friends," Min said.

Zola, Olivia, and Sally gave Min the thumbs-up sign.

"We need you," Tobias moaned. "What did you end up doing last night?"

"Let's just say I was exploring my future options," Min said. "I can't come over."

"Won't you come make us some Minute Rice? Pweese wuff wuff?"

"Make your own Minute Rice," Min said.

"Oh, come on, baby," Tobias said. "Here, Ozzy wants to talk to you. Wuff wuff wuff."

"Hi, Ozzy," Min said into the phone.

Zola, Olivia, and Sally gave Min various looks of disgust.

"Mommy's sorry you're not feewing wuff," Min mumbled, trying to turn her back to the other girls. "Put Daddy back on, okay?"

"If you don't get your ass over here I don't know what I'm going to do. I wuff you," Tobias said. "So are you coming?"

"I don't know." Min looked nervously over her shoulder at the other girls.

"I'm not hanging up until you say you wuff me, too," Tobias said.

Min didn't say anything. He seemed to really need her. And there was a whole side to him that her friends never got to see.

"Well?" Tobias demanded. "I'm going to stay on this phone all day if I have to."

"I wuff you, too," Min said quickly, and hung up the phone.

The girls performed a symphony of vomit sounds. "You can't be serious," Zola said. "You just promised to break up with him two hours ago and you're already going over to his house to be a doggy nurse?"

"They're sick," Min said. "What am I supposed to do?"

"Great," Zola said. "You deserve to have a shitty future." She stormed back into the cafeteria with the other girls behind her. "Oh my God," she said, stunned. There, above their heads, was an eight-foot banner that said, Congratulations to Claudia and Evan, Our Prom Queen and King!

"Just ignore it," Olivia said.

"Sally, lift me up so I can reach it," Zola demanded.

"What? I can't lift you up, Zola," Sally said.

Zola marched over to a table with a geek seated alone at it. "Are you using this chair?" Zola asked. "What am I saying; of course you're not using it." She dragged the chair over to where the banner was, making a horrible nails-on-a-blackboard sound, stood on it, and ripped the banner down onto the cafeteria floor.

Zola flailed around with the thing for a few seconds, looking like a warrior trying to kill a dragon, and stomped on it with her boots. Then she wadded it up and paraded past all the geeks and Hair Net Betty right into the girls' room.

Olivia, Min, and Sally found her in a stall, trying to shove the balled-up banner down the toilet. She flushed the toilet over and over again until it flooded and water poured out onto the bathroom floor.

(Zolar)

Mr. Seidman knocked tentatively on the door to the girls' rest room. "Girls, what's going on in there?"

The girls looked at each other nervously. Zola tried to flush the toilet again, but it just burped up more water.

Mr. Seidman opened the door and took a nervous step inside. He had never been in the girls' room before, but if a situation was developing he would have to take care of it. He stood outside the stall, staring at the toilet with the soggy prom king and queen banner spilling out of it. The floor was covered with water.

"Zolar, this is disgraceful," he said. "I'm very surprised at you girls."

Zola didn't know what to say.

"I want to have a talk with the four of you," he said. A small patch of graffiti that read *Mr. Seidman licks Miss McCormack's hairy pussy* caught his eye. "This isn't the right place for a conversation. Follow me to my office."

Zola, Olivia, Min, and Sally sat on four chairs in Principal Seidman's office. "They didn't do anything," Zola said. "They tried to stop me. It was my fault."

"Well, this is quite serious, Zolar. Destroying school property is a serious offense. I'm going to have to call your father."

"Fine," Zola said. Her father was probably just pouring himself his first glass of grapefruit juice for the morning. Gin and grapefruit, his Sunday morning special.

"I'm very surprised by your attitude, Zolar," Mr. Seidman said.

"Look, I'm sorry I tried to flush the banner but it's not the biggest crime in the world. I think you're making too big of a deal out of this, Mr. Seidman. I mean it's not exactly like I committed the Columbine shootings."

Mr. Seidman's eyebrows shot up to the top of his forehead. "Just saying something like that is a cause for great concern, Zolar," he said.

"It's Zola," Zola said. "Zo-la. La. La. Not lar. La."

Mr. Seidman looked hurt. He turned on the computer and everyone sat in silence while he hit a few keys. It was clear he had no idea how to use it. Finally, after a few minutes, he said, "Zolar, tell me your phone number."

Zola gave him her number and Mr. Seidman dialed. Nothing happened. He hung up and punched in the number again. But still nothing happened.

"You have to dial nine," Zola said.

"Right. Uh, thank you."

Mr. Seidman dialed a third time and this time someone said hello.

"I'm Zola's uncle Clarence," the voice said. "I'm taking care of Zola for a few days."

"I'm afraid you're going to have to come to the school. Zolar has gotten herself into some trouble."

Zola stared gravely at the floor. She thought Mr. Seidman was talking to her father and she was going to be in a lot of trouble when her father came walking through that door. It just made her all the more determined to get even with Claudia. This was all her fault.

Mr. Seidman hung up. "He'll be right over," he said.

They sat in awkward silence while they waited for Zola's father to show up.

But it wasn't her father who walked through the door.

Zola looked up to find Clarence standing there wearing a ridiculous-looking suburban outfit. Red plaid pants and an embarrassing white sweater with little red people golfing on it and white patent leather shoes. He still looked pretty hot, though. Zola suppressed a laugh.

"You must be Zolar's uncle," Mr. Seidman said, extending his hand to Clarence.

Mr. Seidman looked confused. He probably hadn't expected Zola's uncle to be so young, sexy, and black. "Oh, uh, I don't see the family resemblance," Mr. Seidman said.

"Really?" Clarence said. "A lot of people think my niece looks just like me."

"Hi, Uncle Lenny," Zola said.

"It's Uncle Clarence. Clarence Terence. My niece just likes to joke around," Clarence said to Mr. Seidman. "And I'm sure that's what got her into trouble here today."

"Well, I'm afraid Zolar hasn't shown a great deal of school spirit here today," the principal said. "I'm sorry to say her behavior has been a disgrace to our school. There has been a severe banner-flushing incident."

"Zolar, I'm surprised at you," Clarence said. "Her father will be very disappointed to hear about this when he comes home."

"It's a shame to have to make a note of an incident like this on Zolar's permanent record," Mr. Seidman said.

"Yes, that certainly would be a shame," Clarence said. "Perhaps there is something Zolar could do to make it up to you and the other students at La Follette High."

(Sevas)

Zola, Olivia, Min, and Sally donned hair nets and stood behind the lunch counter with Hair Net Betty. Even though there was no one in the cafeteria, there were officially twenty more minutes to go until the end of the prom breakfast, and they would be forced to work behind the counter until the bitter end. And then help with cleanup.

Old man Otis came out of the girls' bathroom and gave Zola a hurt look. He would probably never be able to forgive her for breaking the toilet like that. What kind of a person would try to place an object other than toilet tissue down something so delicate as a newly installed, gleaming white porcelain toilet? Otis would never understand people. He had thought he had seen it all. Over the years he had dealt with flushed report cards, loose-leaf pages, school rings, a lipstick, once even a beeper, but never had there ever been an assault like this.

Perhaps the sign that said, Please Do Not Place

Sanitary Napkins or Paper Towels in Toilet would have to be changed to Sanitary Napkins, Paper Towels, and Banners.

And why was the girls' room always in worse shape than the boys' room? You never saw pee all over the seat in the boys'. And the graffiti! How could these young girls have such filthy minds? Sexual feats he could never even dream of described in precise anatomical detail.

Zola stabbed at the tray of cold toast with a big serving spoon.

"You guys didn't have to do this with me," she said to the other girls.

"We don't mind," Olivia said. She looked the funniest with her hair all wild under her hair net. "Besides, I like wearing this hair net. We can probably get people to start wearing them. We look so cool, everyone in the school will do it. We're starting a major trend."

"This is so fucked up," Min said. "Why don't they just let us start cleaning up now? No one else is going to show up at this stupid thing."

"What am I, chopped liver?" Clarence asked, appearing eagerly at the counter with his orange tray. "Well, well, well, what do we have here? What are those?" he asked, pointing to the cold, dried-out scrambled eggs. "What is that?" he asked, pointing to the sausages. "Some sort of snausage?"

"This is for students only," Hair Net Betty said.

"It's okay," Zola said. "He's my uncle."

"Really?" Hair Net Betty asked, looking Clarence up and down from the top of his cute trendy short dreadlocks to the toes of his shiny white shoes.

"Zola was adopted," Min said. She scraped up some eggs and plopped them down on a plate for Clarence. "Just like me. You'd be surprised to know how many of us are adopted." She said this as though some of the students at La Follette might even be aliens.

"Well, nice to meet you," Hair Net Betty said to Clarence. "I might as well hang up the old apron for the day, since I've got you girls covering for me. Don't forget to double bag the garbage."

Hair Net Betty took off her slippers and put on a pair of sensible shoes. She said good-bye to the girls and left.

"This is an all-new low," Zola said, stabbing a sausage over and over again with a fork. It was quite a violent assault.

"This is good for you girls," Clarence said. "The Hindus call this performing your *seva*. You're giving back to the community. Working to serve your community is part of the spiritual path."

"Did we have to serve our community in public where we could be seen?" Olivia asked.

"These past two days have been one humiliation after another," Zola said.

And then, as if the word *humiliation* were their cue, Evan and Claudia walked into the cafeteria arm in arm. They were still wearing their prom clothes from the night before. They had obviously spent the night together.

Zola ducked as fast as she could behind the counter and curled into a ball on the yellow-and-white tiles of the cafeteria floor. When Claudia saw the three girls in their hair nets, she dragged Evan over to the counter. "Look, our school has three new lunch ladies. Olivia, Sally, and *Mitt,*" Claudia said.

"It's Min," Sally said.

"What are you doing here?" Claudia asked. "Starting off on your careers early? You didn't want to wait until after graduation?"

"We just wanted to perform our *sevas,*" Min said. "We're Hindu now. We're giving back to our community."

"What happened to your hair, Olivia?" Claudia said. Then she noticed Zola on the floor behind the counter, trying to crawl away on her hands and knees. "Zola!" she said. "What are you doing down there? Look, Evan, it's your ex, Zola. Are you a Buddhist, too, Zola? Is that why you're on your knees? You're praying?"

"Cut it out, Claudia," Evan said.

"She dropped a contact lens," Sally said.

"She doesn't even wear contacts," Evan said.

"No, *she* didn't drop it; Min dropped it," Olivia said.

"Then why isn't Min looking for it?" Claudia said.

"Why would Min look for it when she can't even see out of one eye?" Sally said, as if Claudia were the stupidest person on the planet.

"Yeah, I can't see a thing," Min said. "Let me serve you up some yummy eggs." She flung a spoonful of scrambled eggs at Claudia. They landed all over her, but mostly in her cleavage. "Was that your tray?" Min asked.

Zola rose slowly to a standing position. "Found it," she said. She handed the invisible contact lens to Min.

"Thank you," Min said stiffly, holding her hand flat as if she were holding it.

"Hello, Hair Net Zola," Claudia said. She screeched with laughter. "Like, where are your slippers?"

"I think I, like, left them up your ass," Zola said.

Uncle Clarence sat at a table in the corner, watching the scene in complete dismay.

"Hey, where's my banner?" Claudia asked, looking around. "There's always a banner congratulating the queen and king," she whined. "It's supposed to stay up until graduation. Evan, we didn't get our banner with our names written on it."

"Who cares," Evan said, looking flustered. "I don't really want my name on a banner."

Mr. Seidman entered the cafeteria and walked over to the counter to check on the girls. "Zolar, it's nice to see you decided to apologize to Claudiar and Evan for flushing their banner down the toilet," he said.

"What!" Claudia screeched.

Was it her imagination, or did Zola notice a tiny, tiny, barely perceptible smile on Evan's lips? Their eyes met. Zola returned Evan's slight smile with a slight smile of her own.

"She flushed our banner? This is an outrage," Claudia said.

"All right, Claudiar, relax," Mr. Seidman said. "Zolar has promised to paint a new banner and it will be back up by Monday. But Zolar, I do think you owe Claudiar and Evan an apology."

Apologize to Claudia! Zola looked at Clarence for help but he just nodded at her and mouthed, "Say you're sorry."

"I'm sorry, Claudia," Zola said, grimacing. Then she looked at Evan. She could still feel a slight something between them. Something good. "I'm sorry, Evan," she whispered.

"I'm sorry, too," he said, looking deeply into her eyes.

(28)

(The Fugitive)

Min finished wiping down the last table and then got a couple of sausages out of the fridge and ate one of them. Even though they looked totally disgusting she still had to have them.

The other girls had already left, eager to get busy with their plans. Olivia was going to the bookstore. Sally was going underwear shopping. And Zola was upstairs, painting a new banner.

Min was singing "You Don't Own Me" into the other sausage, holding it like a microphone, when Tobias arrived with Ozzy and several pieces of surprisingly expensive, fashionable luggage.

"Hey, Min, thanks a lot for coming to take care of us," he said sarcastically.

Ozzy ran over to Min and she gave him the little sausage microphone.

"He's sick; he can't eat that," Tobias said.

183

"Where did you get that luggage?" Min asked. There was no point in arguing about the sausage.

"From Holden's closet. I stole it," Tobias said, as if it was the most natural thing in the world to steal your roommate's luggage. "The guy's such an asshole. He thinks he's literary because he's named after Holden Caulfield. He's so full of shit."

"You're named after Tobias Wolff," Min said.

"Who's Tobias Wolff?" Tobias asked.

"Never mind," Min said.

Ozzy waddled in a circle and then squatted and waddled again, leaving a trail of diarrhea on the cafeteria floor.

"I told you we're sick," Tobias said, not making any sort of move to clean up the disgusting mess.

"So why did you take the bags?" Min said. She wondered if Tobias was going on a trip. Maybe he was going home to Florida to see his parents. That would be the easiest way to get out of this. She would miss him but some distance was exactly what the two of them needed. She felt bad that she hadn't gone to help him nurse Ozzy. She would have gone if she knew they were going away.

"My roommates kicked me out," Tobias said. "Fucking Holden and Lance. I hate them."

"Why did they kick you out?" Min asked.

"Well, we had a fight because I was watching *Who*

Wants to Be a Millionaire? and they were making fun of Regis and I couldn't concentrate on the questions and then Ozzy made a mess on the floor and they started whining. I went ape shit on them, and they told on me to the dean of students like little babies," Tobias explained.

"What did the dean say?" Min asked.

"It's really no big deal. I just need to find another place to live, that's all."

"It sounds like kind of a big deal to me," Min said. "Whatever happened to those anger management classes, Tobias?"

"Yeah, well, whatever. I'm out."

"So, what are you going to do?"

"I thought I could stay at your house, baby," Tobias said. "Your parents won't mind. I know they probably won't let me stay in your room."

Probably! Min thought. Her parents hated Tobias. He'd hardly ever even *been* in her room.

"But I could stay down in that fancy rumpus room of yours and you could sneak down for a little cuddle in the middle of the night."

That would be fun, Min thought before she could stop herself. She wondered if she had made up her mind too quickly to dump Tobias. It had been a very emotional twenty-four hours and she hadn't had a moment to think. She loved him and he loved her. And if he stayed at her house for a day or two she might be able to sort out her feelings for him.

"All right," Min said meekly. "But just for a few days until you find a new apartment." She couldn't just let him sleep in the streets. But she couldn't let Zola, Olivia, and Sally know about it, either. For the next few days it would be like housing a fugitive. It *would* be fun.

Old man Otis came out of the girls' room with his mop and bucket on wheels and stopped short when he saw the mess Ozzy had left in the middle of the cafeteria floor. He couldn't even speak. He just stood there shaking his head in disgust.

(29)

(Barely There)

"I think I'll go to the mall with you," Olivia said to Sally when they got out to the parking lot. "They have a bookstore there, right? And I promise I'll walk right by the hair salon without even *looking* in." She pulled out her compact and a lipstick from her purse and applied the lipstick expertly.

"Why do you need to wear makeup to study?" Sally asked.

"I'm not studying," Olivia said. "I'm *researching*. Didn't you see *Erin Brockovich*? Just because I'm going to be more serious now doesn't mean I have to look like a nun. A lot of serious women wear lipstick. Anyway, it was just a reflex action." She tugged at her turtleneck and then rolled it up at the bottom so that her belly button showed. "God, this thing's hot."

They drove for a while and then Sally suddenly asked Olivia, "Have you ever kissed a girl?"

"What?" Olivia said, shocked. "Why?" Olivia couldn't believe what she was hearing. Was Sally gay? Was that why she was always so uncomfortable and idiotic around boys?

"I'm just curious," Sally said. "No reason." She wanted to tell Olivia about Zola kissing her on prom night, but she didn't want to betray Zola. She was still her friend.

"I've never kissed a girl," Olivia said. "But I don't think there's anything wrong with it," she added quickly. If Sally wanted to tell her that she was a lesbian she didn't want her to feel that she would be judged. It was okay with Olivia if Sally felt ready to come out of the closet. It's funny, you could know someone almost your whole life and not know them at all.

"No, I don't think there's anything wrong with it, either," Sally said. "Do you think *Zola's* ever done it with a girl?"

"Done it?" Olivia said. What was this about? Did Sally have a crush on Zola?

Sally started to blush. "You know, do you think she might be . . ." Sally didn't even know how to put this. She had never had a conversation like this in her life and she felt way out of her league. "Do you think she might be . . . *bi?*"

Olivia laughed. "I really don't think so, Sally. She could have any girl or guy in the school but I think she's only had the guys. What made you say that, anyway?"

"I don't know," Sally said. "Forget I said anything."

"All right," Olivia said. Maybe Sally was just nervous about losing her virginity and thought it might be easier if she did it with a girl. Did that even count? Olivia wondered to herself.

They circled the mall parking lot, looking for a space.

"Hmmm, does being a virgin count as a handicap?" Olivia asked as they passed the empty handicapped spaces.

"I don't think so," Sally mumbled, annoyed.

"Can I help you?" a salesgirl asked Sally.

"I'm fine," Sally said, picking up a pair of black silk panties from a giant pile of them.

Just being in Victoria's Secret made Sally uncomfortable. She felt like everyone was staring at her. She wished Clarence Terence would come and make her invisible.

Olivia had gone on to the bookstore, leaving Sally with the wisdom that she couldn't lose with a matching bra-and-panties set. Sally had decided to forgo the days-of-the-week underpants. They were childish, Olivia said. That was the old, girlish Sally, not the new, womanly Sally.

The salesgirl didn't go away. She was incredibly tall

and skinny. Sally now understood the meaning of the expression "tits on a stick."

"Do these come with a matching bra?" Sally asked, holding up the silk panties.

The salesgirl looked Sally up and down. Especially up. "They do, but I might recommend something with a little more support."

What was that supposed to mean? Sally wondered.

The salesgirl handed Sally the strangest bra she had ever seen. It had liquid pouches built into the cups. Like water balloons. "Why don't you give this a try?" the salesgirl said.

Sally took the bra into the dressing room and tried it on. It made her breasts look enormous. They floated up under her chin. She really couldn't get much sexier than this, she decided.

She vogued in front of the mirror, putting her hands on her bent knees, pushing out her chest, and laughing flirtatiously like Marilyn Monroe in *Bus Stop*. She was like a hot fudge sundae, a pool of water on a hot day, a fluffy feather bed. Utterly irresistible.

Still dressed in the aqua bra, Sally sat down on the little bench in the dressing room. She pulled out her diary and began writing all about what would happen when her dream boy saw her in her new bra.

I'll make him close his eyes. Then, when I count to

ten, I'll be standing over him in this bra. We won't even talk. Not until afterward. I'll run my hands over his dreadlocks and he'll tell me about all the places he's been. . . .

Clarence paced outside the dressing room impatiently. He wanted to pull back the curtain and order Sally to put her diary down and get with the program, but he didn't want her to think he was some sort of horny ladies' lingerie stalker. He wanted to make her words disappear, just to freak her out, so she would start living in real time instead of making up silly stories about boys with dreadlocks. . . .

Clarence ducked behind a rack of Barely There seamless bras and blushed. Oh God. Sally was writing about him! He'd thought he fixed that. Now there was no way he was going in there. She would probably try to kiss him again. Clarence had learned that generosity was the true path to spiritual enlightenment, but this was taking it too far. He walked quickly toward the Victoria's Secret exit, tucking a pair of black silk boxers into his pocket as he went.

Meanwhile, in the bookstore, Olivia was bewitched by the boy with the gorgeous dimples browsing in the study-aids section. He was flipping through an LSAT preparation book and he had a guide to law schools under one of his extremely cut arms.

Olivia walked over to where he was standing and pretended to look at the books in that section.

"Cool glasses," the boy said.

"Thanks," Olivia said. "Do you know where I could find an LSAT prep book?" she asked him, patting her poofy hair. Oh, why hadn't she blow-dried it straight this morning?

"I've got one right here," the boy said, holding up the book.

"Wow," she said. "We both need the same book."

She had never considered law school before but it was actually a really great idea. If she studied hard in college and ended up going to a great law school then she definitely wouldn't end up being a stewardess schlepping barf bags and chicken thumbs for a living. She could be a serious lawyer and still meet hot men like this one.

"I'm Holden," he said, putting out his hand.

"Olivia Dawes," she said seriously, taking his hand and engaging in the firm, self-assured, and earnest handshake of a future United States Supreme Court Judge.

("Freebird")

Zola sat miserably in the art room, wearing an incredibly dorky purple smock. Instead of being out there plotting how she was going to get even with Claudia Choney, she was stuck making a new congratulations banner for her.

She procrastinated for an hour and then finally pulled a long strip of brown paper from a giant roll and cut it with the orange-handled scissors. Congratulations, Claudia, for Stealing My Boyfriend, the banner should say. Congratulations, Claudia, on Being a Bitch. Congratulations, Claudia, on Being a Skank Whore.

Zola laid the strip of paper on the newspapers she had put down on the floor and weighed the curling ends down with books. Then she opened a big jar of red paint and found a brush.

Maybe she should just write, *Evan and Zola Forever*.

With paint spattering she wrote a giant *F.* A few minutes later Fuck You, Claudia, was taking up the length of the paper banner.

Just then Olivia and Sally walked in with their Borders and Victoria's Secret shopping bags. When they saw Zola's creation they laughed. But Zola could tell they were worried that she was seriously considering hanging up the banner.

"It looks like we got here just in time," Sally said.

Olivia and Sally helped Zola make a new banner. Congratulations, Clawdia and Evan, Our Prom Queen and King. Maybe no one would notice that Zola had misspelled Claudia's name. After all, it was a mistake anyone could have made.

They carried the banner down to the cafeteria and stood on stools, using a staple gun to hang it on the wall. Upside down. That, too, was a mistake anyone could have made.

Zola, Olivia, and Sally drove in silence toward Min's house. Zola was in the driver's seat with Olivia next to her, looking out the window, trying not to think about Holden or Bill. But which one was cuter?

Sally was writing in her diary. She couldn't wait to put her new bra back on and try it out.

Zola pressed on the gas.

She went faster and faster.

"Hey, slow down," Olivia said.

"I'm so mad," Zola said.

A siren sounded behind them.

"Shit," Zola said. "I'm going to get a speeding ticket."

We are being pulled over, Sally wrote.

After a few seconds, Zola pulled the car over and waited. Maybe they could flirt themselves out of this one.

A pudgy yellow-headed cop approached. He took off his sunglasses like Erik Estrada in *CHiPs* and bent over to look into the car. Actually, he was more like the blond one. What was that guy's name? Which one was Poncherello? Zola wondered.

Zola looked at his name tag. Officer Shawn. "I'm really sorry I was going so fast, Officer Shawn," Zola said, smiling sweetly at the cop. "My friend in the backseat is pregnant and she's feeling really sick. I was trying to get her home."

Sally turned red. She didn't look at all pregnant, sitting there with her Victoria's Secret shopping bag.

"Do you need assistance, ma'am?" Officer Shawn asked, peering at the pregnant woman in the backseat.

Just then, Clarence Terence roared up on his bike. He stomped on the brake and whipped off his shades. He was slightly winded and there were circles under his eyes. Sally wanted to jump on the back of his bike and ride off into the sunset. They could go to Mexico and live on the beach in a grass shack and she'd wear nothing but her new Victoria's Secret bra and panties all day.

"I'll handle this," Clarence said, winking at the girls.

Officer Shawn couldn't believe it. It was the same nutcase rock star dude who had gotten away the day before. He was really asking for it.

"Well, well, well," Officer Shawn said. "If it isn't the Wicked Witch of the West. Are you having a nice time in Oz? You want me to take you somewhere safe and dry for the night? We keep it locked to keep all the bad guys in."

Clarence pulled out his guitar and began to play "Freebird" very slowly. He picked a long song on purpose since it might take a while to get rid of this guy. After playing a few chords he took his hand off the strings and flapped it at Zola, cueing her to make her getaway.

But Zola was already hip to his groove. She hadn't even cut the engine. "Uh, Officer. I don't think we can wait around. I have to get my friend to the hospital," she said.

Officer Shawn was much more interested in locking up this weirdo on the motorcycle than in giving these four teenagers a speeding ticket. "All right," he said. "I'll let you girls go this time, but I don't want to see you speeding again."

"Uh, we won't. Thank you," Zola said. She drove the

car away slowly, batting her eyelashes at Clarence as they pulled away.

Officer Shawn watched the car until it was out of sight. He hoped they would be all right. Especially that little redhead in the backseat. She was much too young to be pregnant. He wondered if she was going to keep her baby.

When he turned back to the dope on the motorcycle, he was gone. A few bars of "Freebird" still hung in the air.

(31)

(Start Here)

Zola, Olivia, and Sally knocked on the Weinstocks' door. When it opened, they were surprised to see Tobias standing there holding Ozzy, eating a sandwich, and wearing Min's doggy bathrobe. It barely covered what they really didn't want to see.

"Are you holding Min hostage or something?" Zola asked.

"No, actually we're living together," Tobias said. He headed back into the kitchen. "She's in the shower," he said over his shoulder.

Zola started up the stairs with Sally and Olivia behind her. They stormed into Min's room and right into her bathroom.

Min screamed. "You scared me," she said. She turned off the shower and wrapped herself in a towel. "I guess you saw Tobias down there," she said. "He really needed a place to stay. I didn't know what to do."

"Lenny never told us what we were supposed to do," Sally said wistfully. "He just showed us our miserable futures and left the rest up to us."

"Do we have to discuss this in here?" Min asked.

The girls piled out of the bathroom and into the bedroom. There, sprawled out on Min's bed and wearing an ice eye mask, was Clarence Terence. His shoes and socks were lined up neatly on the floor next to the bed.

"You could at least knock," Min said.

"Lenny, what should we do?" Sally asked, sitting on the bed at his feet.

"You girls are very high maintenance, you know that?" Clarence said.

"It's just that we're already doing everything wrong," Zola said.

"Hmmm," Clarence said. "My feet are awfully sore. Would one of you mind rubbing them with some of that cucumber lotion on Min's dresser?"

"And you think *we're* high maintenance?" Zola asked.

Sally got the lotion, squirted some into her hand, and started massaging his feet. She had never touched a man's feet before. It made her dizzy.

"You know, a future takes a lifetime to create," Clarence said. "You can't just change it in a day."

The girls breathed a collective sigh of relief. They could start again tomorrow. Thank God for Clarence.

They really should have trusted him more. He was their fairy godmother, after all.

"But don't forget," Clarence added. "Every time you turn a corner something could happen that could change your life forever."

"Doesn't that contradict what you just said about not being able to change things in a day?" Zola asked.

Clarence sighed. "I suppose so. But life is filled with contradictions."

"Just tell us where to start," Sally said.

Clarence thought for a moment. He sat up and pulled off his eye mask. "Start here," he said, putting his hand on his heart.